Horses of God

Horses of God

MAHI BINEBINE
Translated by Lulu Norman

Tin House Books
Portland, Oregon & New York, New York

First published in France as *Les étoiles de Sidi Moumen* by Flammarion 2010

First published in Great Britain by Granta Books 2013

Copyright © 2010 by Flammarion
Translation copyright © 2013 by Lulu Norman

First North American edition published by Tin House Books 2013

Published by Tin House Books, Portland, Oregon, and New York, New York
Distributed to the trade by Publishers Group West, 1700 Fourth St., Berkeley, CA 94710, www.pgw.com

Library of Congress Cataloging-in-Publication Data
Binebine, Mahi.
[Étoiles de Sidi Moumen. English]
Horses of god / Mahi Binebine ; translated by Lulu Norman.
    p. cm.
ISBN 978-1-935639-53-4
1. Young men—Morocco—Casablanca—Fiction. 2. Islamic fundamentalism—Fiction. I. Norman, Lulu. II. Title.
PQ3989.2.B534E8613 2013
843'.914—dc23
                                        2012033965

Interior design by Jakob Vala
Printed in the USA
www.tinhouse.com

For Claude Durand

1

YOU MIGHT WALK right past our part of town without ever suspecting it was there. A high, crenellated
adobe wall separates it from the boulevard, where an
uninterrupted stream of cars makes an unholy din. In
this wall we'd hollowed clefts like arrow slits so we
could freely contemplate the other world. When I was
a kid our favorite game was to pour bowls of piss on
to rich passersby, biting our lips as they cursed, yelled
insults, and looked up at the sky. My brother Hamid
was our leader; he rarely missed his target. We'd watch
him do his stuff, stifling our laughter, which, seconds
after the golden shower, would burst out uncontrol-
lably. We'd be jubilant, rolling around in the dust like
puppies. Ever since the day a stone thrown by a furious victim hit my head, I was never quite the same. At
least that's what everyone around me thought; that's

what had been drummed into me nonstop since I was little. I ended up accepting it and, eventually, quite liking it. All my escapades were half forgiven on account of that handicap. But I was no stupider than anyone else. In soccer, everyone will tell you, I was the slum's best goalie. My idol's name was Yachine. The legendary Yachine. I never saw him in action but there were so many stories . . . Some claimed he could stop a ball fired from a Krupp cannon, others that his body defied the laws of gravity. People even said that his premature death had been plotted by international strikers, put to shame by his talent. Whatever the truth, I wanted to be Yachine or nothing. So I changed my name to his. Yemma didn't like it, but since I refused to answer to the name for which a lamb had been sacrificed in front of our shack, she'd had to get used to it. Only my father, who'd always been old and stubborn, kept on with the outdated "Moh." You're not going to get very far with a name like that.

In any case, I didn't hang around in life too long because there wasn't a lot to do. And I have to say right now: I'm not sorry to be done with it. I don't have the slightest nostalgia for the eighteen or so years of misery that were my lot. Although at first, in the days straight after my death, I'd have found it hard to say no to those biscuits my mother used to make with salty butter, her honey cakes or spiced coffee. Still, those earthly needs slowly faded and even the memory of them eventually vanished too, eroded by my new status as a ghost. If in the odd moment of weakness I still think of Yemma stroking me as she rooted around in my hair, getting rid of the nits, I say to myself: "Get a grip, Yachine, your head's been blown to smithereens. Where could the nits go burrowing if you no longer have any hair?" No, I'm glad to be a long way from the corrugated iron, the cold, the sewers spilling their guts, and all the putrid stench of my childhood. I won't describe where I am now because I don't know myself. All I can say is that I'm reduced to an entity that, to use the language of down below, I'll call consciousness: that is to say, the restful outcome of myriad lucid thoughts. Not the dark, narrow ones that dogged my brief existence, but thoughts with aspects that are infinite, iridescent, sometimes dazzling.

2

LONG BEFORE EVERYONE had a satellite dish, inge-
nious contraptions made out of couscous pots sprout-
ed over all the roofs of our neighborhood, enabling
us to watch foreign programs. To be honest, the images were blurred, almost scrambled, but you could
just about see the outlines and the sound was more
or less okay. We'd mostly watch the Spanish and Por-
tuguese channels for the soccer, German for the porn
(the poor image quality at least made the brutish look
erotic), and the Arab channels for our daily dose of the
Israeli-Palestinian conflict and the evil doings of the
man-eating West. Since color TV was beyond the reach
of most of His Majesty's subjects, we had a strip of
colored plastic film that we stuck over the screen: three
horizontal bands, azure on top, poetically evoking the
sky, pale yellow in the middle, and grass green below.

This meant we saw the flickering images through mul-
ticolored plastic, which was often scratched and grubby. Also, because my father was deaf, we'd turn up the
volume so loud that we'd have to watch the same channel as our neighbors so as not to be disruptive. In spite
of all that, young and old would come together every
evening around this magical screen, brazenly open to
the wonders of the world.

If Casablanca had had a record book, Yemma would
have been right up there: fourteen pregnancies in
fourteen years! Can anyone top that? And eleven had
lived. All boys. If the twins hadn't been struck down
by meningitis at the age of three, we could have made
up the soccer team all by ourselves: the Stars of Sidi
Moumen, pride and joy of the neighborhood. We'd
have made all the teams from the other slums quake.
And Yachine, yours truly, regular goalkeeper, would
have been its unbreachable defense. We'd have been so
famous that even people from the rich parts of town
would have risked climbing the wall to come and cheer
us on. Who knows, the town dump might have become a real soccer field. Perhaps not with turf like the
stadiums of the big teams, but at least an open space,
rid of the revolting mounds of rubbish. And as for the
people that make their living from them, well, tough;
they'd just have to go scavenging elsewhere. It's not as
if there's a shortage of dumps. That said, poor as we

were, Yemma banned us from working at the dump. There was no escaping the sniffing session when we got home at night. If you stank of rubbish, you were in for it. Our mother had made a formidable whip that she kept hanging by the door. And as for bringing anything home, no chance. She delighted in destroying it then and there. Still, we'd find stuff at the dump. Hamid was the only one who dared to defy our mother. Incapable of doing without hashish, he'd resigned himself to paying the price each day. And though he was careful to wash himself all over at the street pump, he'd still reek of his crime. Yemma could thrash him all she liked, he carried on. He had to have his fix, his expensive tobacco, and his rolling papers.

I can modestly say that of all the scavengers at the dump, Hamid was the most gifted. He had almost a sixth sense for unearthing the rare pearl. Combined with precocious intelligence, this animal instinct instantly placed him ahead of the pack. He knew exactly which district any particular garbage truck came from, and he didn't stint on bribes for the drivers in return for information. So, rather than foraging blindly like most people, he'd search methodically. By the age of twelve, he was already employing one kid to clean and repair his booty and another to sell it off at the flea market at a price he'd set in advance. I was fascinated by my brother Hamid. He protected me. And spoiled me. He could turn violent if anyone started on me. One evening, I remember it like yesterday, he beat to death a neighbor who'd dragged me over toward the cesspools, way behind the dump. Though we'd only been playing, imitating Bollywood heroes. Morad was having a laugh, nibbling my ears, whispering weird words. His rough tongue gave me the shivers. He'd pinned my hands to the ground to stop me from running away. His curly hair smelled of olive oil. And tasted like it too; my mouth was full of it. Morad's tickling was making me laugh so much I didn't hear Hamid, who suddenly appeared, like a ghost. But instead of throwing himself into the fray he stood still, stiff as a rod. I didn't notice the stone he was holding, because the night was black. When Morad cried out, I thought he was still singing. I don't know why Hamid struck him so hard, on the head. The blood started gushing down his face and I was so scared I wanted to scream. I couldn't. My screams stayed inside me, as if they'd been sucked in by my belly. I tried opening my mouth; nothing came out. In a daze, I looked at my brother, who was trembling, his fists clenched. I knew I'd get it next. Wearing those lethal boots with the crampons he'd picked up on the dump, he kicked my ass, calling me a fag and other insults I don't even dare repeat. I told him that we were only playing, we hadn't hurt anyone. But he was wild with rage. It was as if his anger, amplified by the darkness, was a battalion of devils brandishing their pitchforks, ready to stab me. My brother could sometimes be unfair, it's true. And yet he loved me; he'd have done anything for me. I was angry with him about Morad, but that's all in the past now.

I never went near the cesspools again. Obviously I couldn't hang out with Morad any longer, because he hadn't survived my brother's attack. He'd been buried in the dump. Hamid knew every nook and cranny of it. No one went foraging on that side anymore. It was old garbage, passed a thousand times through the sieve of human despair. At first I refused to believe my friend was dead. But I ended up forgetting him. Well, not completely. The few times I let in a goal at soccer and went off to fetch the ball, I couldn't help glancing at the exact spot where my friend lay decomposing. One evening, I felt brave enough to go and check if he was still there. On top of the mound I'd located thanks to the white carcass of a dog shriveled by the scorching heat, I used a stick to scrape away the sludge he'd been buried in. Maybe Morad had survived my brother's assault after all. Perhaps he'd just pretended to be dead so Hamid would stop hitting him, and had stood up right after we'd gone and left the slum. Perhaps he'd disappeared purely to give us a fright, to punish us. So I dug, first with the stick and then with my hands, which was easier. The natural stench of the dump overpowered that of the corpse. When I saw a finger sticking out of the mud between two food cans, I ran off as fast as I could, not turning round, because I thought Morad's ghost was after me. I only stopped when I reached Omar the coalman's shop. A paraffin lamp made a halo of light round the hunched figures of ex-soldiers who congregated there to play checkers. My heart was thudding, I was trembling all over. Just thinking about it would give me goose bumps if I still inhabited my skin.

From then on, I decided to fall in line and believe, like everyone else, that Morad had fled the slum to fend for himself in the city, like so many kids his age. Believe that he'd come back someday, his pockets so full that his parents would soon forget he'd run away and even encourage him to go off again and carry on. With hindsight, now that I'm up here, I'm not angry with my brother anymore. I tell myself that in a sense he did Morad a favor, in the same way that Abu Zoubeir did me one, except he didn't hit me with a stone. His weapons were different, more devastating. But I'll tell you about that later. Because Abu Zoubeir is very much alive. And still hanging out in a so-called garage with other half-starved wretches like me.

3

WITH HIS CHESTNUT hair and green eyes, Nabil should have been born somewhere else. He looked so unlike the rest of us. Without his rags, on feast days, you'd have sworn he was from the other world. A reverse immigrant, one of those crusaders fresh from the North, come to rub up against our poverty, like the hippies. Yet he was definitely one of us. We'd grown up in the same filth, waded through the same sludge. He got his good looks from his mother, Tamu, a prostitute who'd decided to devote her charms to the layabouts of Sidi Moumen. A champion of cheap sex, she saw herself as providing a public service, and charged rates that were near communist. Tamu commanded particular respect in our neighborhood as well as in the surrounding slums. Some say she could have plied her trade anywhere, even in the rich parts of town, had she bothered to scrub up a bit.

Enlivened by her gold teeth, Tamu's luminous features exuded carnivorous charm. The eighty kilos of creamy flesh filling her satin djellabas drove men crazy as she walked by. She also worked as a singer on occasion, at weddings, baptisms, and circumcision ceremonies, and she sang so well that, despite their misgivings, the neighborhood women would eventually seek her out. Not one to bear grudges, and conscious of her talent, Tamu readily agreed to make an appearance in the most hostile of shacks. For spicing up a party she had no equal. She'd launch herself body and soul among the guests, tambourine under her arm and buttocks twitching as if an electric current had shot through her; fluttering her eyelids like a Hindu dancer, she'd slay one man and then the next, as her piercing voice rang out through the loudspeakers set up on the roof, spreading happiness into all the surrounding hovels.

Nabil lived alone with his mother in an isolated shack near the street pump. He'd spend the day outdoors because his mother saw her clients at home. That's why he'd be the first to show up at the dump and would only leave after dark. He worked for my brother Hamid, who treated him fairly. He protected him too. Woe betide anyone who dared to call him the son of a whore! Hamid, who was handy with his fists, would instantly pummel the guilty party. Anyway, after Morad disappeared, Nabil and I became inseparable. Sometimes I'd help him out at the dump, picking up bones, bits of glass, and metal. Occasionally I'd turn up a ram horn, which was highly prized at the souk because it was used to make combs. I'd also skin the rubber from wires, to get to the copper. If he lent me his knife, I could make ten balls of it a day. Nabil had to fill the three burlap sacks that my brother would supply every morning. And he'd do it in style; whether the rain beat down or the wind blew a gale, the sacks were ready and tied up neatly by dusk. A wooden cart, dragged along by a skeletal mule with a one-eyed old man at the reins, made the rounds to collect them. Hamid no longer even bothered to come and check if the work had been done by the book. He trusted Nabil. He said that he was no cheat, unlike those other punks, who'd lie around sniffing glue all day. Although Nabil was better paid than the rest of them, money ran through his fingers, so he never saved any. He'd often invite me to share his tin of sardines, his barley bread, and a big bottle of Coca-Cola. We'd sit down in a shelter he'd built out of planks and cardboard and treat ourselves to a feast, talking about the city we'd go and visit one day. His mother had described it to him in fabulously lavish detail. I don't think he was making it up. The only time I was able to go there was the last time, when everything in my mind was so muddled.

Nabil dreamed of transforming his shelter into a real house. He already had the whole thing planned out: two bedrooms, a corner for the kitchen, and a living room. As for a toilet, he'd do what everyone else did: go and relieve himself at the dump. But for the moment his project was difficult to get off the ground. Every time he picked up some corrugated iron, or a beam in good condition, it would be stolen. Still, he didn't give up hope. I promised to help him the day he started seriously planning the work. My brother Hamid said much the same: "We businessmen must stick together." He suggested an empty hut for storing Nabil's materials: plastic, branches, bricks, girders—anything, in fact, that might help us build a roof that didn't leak and could withstand the lashing of the wind and other bad weather.

Nabil would dream. He used to say that the day I felt the need to stand on my own two feet, I could come and live with him. We'd have a brazier and a big pot for cooking up succulent tagines. It was only a question of time. If we worked hard and persevered, we'd get there. That was when I started to feel cramped at home. We slept six to a room no bigger than a cellar. I couldn't stand the snoring, or the mixture of barely identifiable odors: the stink of shoes, sweat, pants, the DDT powder that Yemma did her best to spread under the raffia sleeping mats every night. Yes, I too began to dream of a room of my own. Of a real bed with a box spring that no scorpion could scale, nor any other creature, except maybe ticks, which never really bothered me. In any case, I much preferred them to the suffocating smell of insecticide. There wouldn't be mothballs in my room either. I don't know why Yemma was so concerned about moths; we had so little wool, so few clothes, that our hovel would have been the last place they'd go to feast. But Yemma was like that. The cleanest, shrewdest woman I ever had the good fortune to meet. Early each morning she'd begin by waking one of us to go and fetch water from the pump, though she'd spare the little ones. It took several trips to fill the big earthenware jar. She'd splash water over the yard in a kind of daily war against dust. Next she'd water the pots of basil that stood at the entrance to the bedrooms, to keep out mosquitoes. Finally, she'd fill the kettle to boil water for us to wash with, and set about preparing the breakfast we'd all have together. She loved watching us eat. She'd fuss over each of us like a mother hen. We were her men. Nine strong lads and a father who'd decided to be old before his time, crouched in his corner, endlessly fingering his amber prayer beads. He prayed sitting down because he claimed he no longer had the strength to stand. He, the former quarry worker, had become so thin, so desiccated, just like the wasteland that had once been the industrial district, where he'd always lived. Yemma would serve him his soup and plump up the cushions behind his back without a word. Then she'd look over our clothes like a corporal

inspecting his squad: a button missing from a shirt, a
sock or jumper with holes in it would trigger an ava-
lanche of reproach: "What! Are you trying to make
me a laughingstock?" Or "Come on! You take that off
immediately, I'm not dead yet!" And she'd grab the
sewing basket. "Yachine," she'd call out, "come over
and thread this needle for me, you're the one with the
best eyes." I was so happy to have something that was
better than the others. I'd moisten the thread between
my lips and slip it through the eye first time. Yemma
smiled at me. I loved seeing her smile.

Some days, Nabil would turn up on our doorstep at
dawn. As soon as Yemma heard his whistle (that was his
way of calling me), she'd dunk a crust of hot bread in the
plate of olive oil and say: "Here, give this to your friend."
Looking hungry, his smile as wide as his ears, Nabil took
it gratefully. He'd ask me for a glass of water to rinse out
his mouth because in Sidi Moumen our teeth grated
continuously, due to the dust that got everywhere. Then
he'd wolf down the hunk of bread before he went to
work. Nabil was no poorer than us, far from it. It was
just that his bohemian mother was in the habit of sleeping in. She worked so late that getting up early was out
of the question. To avoid waking her, he'd sneak out like
a thief, on tiptoe. I have no idea how anyone could sleep
with the garbage trucks' morning racket anyway. But
around there, everyone got used to everything—to the

stench of rotting and death, for instance, which became so familiar and clung to our skin. We couldn't smell it anymore. And if it were suddenly, magically, to vanish, Sidi Moumen would lose its soul. The air would probably seem bland and insipid; dogs and cats would vanish from the scene, as would the hordes of seagulls that besieged the place, preferring its contaminated, sweltering heat to sea air, its shadowy foragers to fishermen of the deep. Even the old people would be bored if there were no more flies to swat away, or mosquitoes or anything. Can you imagine: Sidi Moumen, stripped bare! Without its wild nights at the dump. Without its campfires, where random musicians, their petrol cans transformed into mandolins, unfurl their laments into a hashish-scented sky; and those fields of plastic bags that sing in the wind, while the teasing half-light turns the rubbish dunes into infinite beaches . . .

What? I'm rambling! Well, so what? What else can I do now that I'm consumed with loneliness and, like a strange ghost, skulk around my childhood memories? I'm not ashamed to tell you I was sometimes happy in that hideous squalor, in the filth of that accursed cesspit; yes, I was happy in Sidi Moumen, my home.

4

OF ALL THE Stars of Sidi Moumen, only Fuad was able to go to school, which was a few kilometers from the shantytown. He lived in an outhouse of the mosque where his father performed various duties: muezzin, caretaker, imam, as well as other more unpleasant but no less lucrative chores, such as laying out corpses, exorcizing the possessed (or presumed possessed), or reading the Koran at the cemetery. Fuad lived for only one thing: playing soccer with us, which he was categorically forbidden to do. Yet he was unquestionably a born striker; he alone could make the difference in a big tournament. As soon as he could escape his father's clutches, he'd be back in the team, and the matches would be unforgettable. But Fuad was forever scanning the sky, because once he'd been caught right in the middle of the dump: from the top of his minaret, the muezzin had spotted him as we waded through the muck after a ball. I can still see Fuad now, petrified, almost fainting, the second the cranky loudspeaker sputtered his name. His father's voice was unique and impossible to mistake, since we heard it five times a day. A shrill, artificial voice that made you want to do anything except go and pray. I reckon Fuad wet himself, knowing a beating was inescapable. In any case, after that incident, he disappeared from the scene for a long time. He'd been completely banned from going anywhere near us. And even from leaving home, except to go to school. We'd sometimes see him in the morning, his satchel on his back, being dragged along by his uncle like a condemned man to the scaffold. He'd shoot us a sideways glance, enviously, sending subtle signals to find out the results of the matches we were playing without him. If his uncle noticed, a vengeful slap would fall like lightning on his face. He'd growl at him, calling us every name under the sun. Under normal circumstances, a stone would have been sent flying through the air toward that creep. Hamid was a mean shot with his catapult. But he held off, so as not to make more trouble for Fuad.

So several months went by and the Stars were a bit lackluster. We continued with our brutal confrontations every Sunday, and the rest of the week we'd all go back to our normal lives. Nabil had joined the team and was doing pretty well. He'd finally built his shack, a humbler construction than originally planned, but we'd gotten used to it, since it was now our headquarters. All the Stars would meet there to work out match tactics. Nabil was happy he'd left his family home, though his mother still visited several times a week. She'd bring him a basket crammed with food that we'd all feast on. She wouldn't stay long, since she knew her presence embarrassed him, especially if we were there. My brother Hamid had graciously donated a paraffin lamp and a radio-cassette player he'd unearthed in almost working order. We'd had it repaired for next to nothing, polished it, and placed it on an upturned crate in the middle of the room. What nights we'd spend in that shack, all huddled together, listening to Berber songs from the Middle Atlas and the furious rhythms of Nass el Ghiwane. Smoking spliffs, dreaming up fantastic stories . . .

To our great joy, one fine Sunday in July, we spied Fuad on top of a mound of garbage in his soccer getup—meaning bare-chested, wearing plastic sandals—waving his bony arms: he was back, with no explanation, to reclaim his place as center forward, which no one was in any position to contest. It was only a week later that we found out about his father, who'd been struck down by a stroke that paralyzed his left side, invading his face to the point that he couldn't speak—which is unfortunate for a muezzin. Fuad's uncle had taken over the role straightaway. As the eldest male, Fuad quite naturally became head of the family. He wasn't yet fourteen. But being head had significant advantages: he immediately stopped school, had a mobile stall built, and began to sell cakes made by his mother and his sister, Ghizlane. He'd grown up overnight, though his puny body hadn't followed suit. Not much taller than a twelve-year-old, he had thin, bandy legs and an angular face that was swallowed up by his African features, and he always wore the somber expression of those who are born to be unhappy. Despite that, on a soccer field, it was as if no one else existed. We were proud to count him one of us. He and I were the pillars of the team; our combined talents warranted its glittering name.

We had many rivals; every slum had a team. The "Chichane" (which means Chechnya) shantytown had its Lions; "Tqalia" (guts) its Eagles; "Toma"—named after a Frenchwoman who was said to have had coffee there once—had its Tomahawks; scariest of all were the players from the village of stones: the Serpents of Douar Lahjar, the only ones who had a hope against us. On Sundays we'd assemble at the dump for legendary matches that would usually end in gladiatorial combat: ruthless fights that left everyone pretty mashed up. Still, we couldn't stop ourselves going back for more the following week. We needed to square up to each other,

smash a ball, or someone's face. It gave us relief. Truth to
tell, my brother Hamid was often waiting nearby. He'd
protect me with a bicycle chain he wore as a belt, which
he'd whip out in a flash if there was any trouble. If it did
kick off, I'd hide behind him and nothing bad could
happen to me; I'd emerge unscathed, apart from a few
scratches or a black eye at worst. Hamid used to collect
scars on my account, because other boys were frustrated
and jealous of the way I played. My genius for stopping impossible balls earned me thundering applause.
Countless Serpents, Eagles, and Tomahawks wanted me
dead. Poor Fuad, though, had no one to defend him;
he had nothing but his legs. He'd often get caught and
seriously beaten up. Like Hamid, he'd amassed an impressive number of injuries. What he was most afraid
of was the inevitable visit to the barber, who doubled
as a bonesetter. That man was a nasty piece of work,
who'd reset our bones with brute force. It was his way
of punishing us. Most of the time we'd lose consciousness at some point. We could have wreaked revenge on
that wild-eyed maniac, but we knew that sooner or later
we'd be back in his dreaded grip . . . One day his shop
was burnt to the ground; the culprit was never caught.
Still, in Sidi Moumen, a hovel in flames isn't exactly the
end of the world. It gets rebuilt the same day and people
rally round, offering the victim mats, blankets, clothes,
and stuff for the kitchen. And life carries on as normal.

The only deliberate fire I was lucky enough to witness from beginning to end was the police-station fire. After the police had left a young dealer for dead, the decision was unanimous. Boys brought gas cans and set fire to the building. They were raging against "the Doberman," a corrupt detective, a brute, a piece of filth washed up among us, who bullied people and sucked their blood. That scumbag lorded it over the anthill of small-time dealers and other thieves who made their living in Sidi Moumen. No van filled with hashish or smuggled goods could get inside the wall without his taking a cut. He also had an efficient network of informers, so nothing escaped him. He knew the innards of all the shacks and had detailed files on all of us. If some poor wretch attempted to complain, he'd confront him with the crimes of his closest friends or family, because most of Sidi Moumen's inhabitants have skeletons in their cupboards. As the years went by, people's resentment grew fiercer, swelling like the waters of a stream about to burst its banks. So, that night, in a surge of anger, the street caught fire like a powder keg. Omar the coalman's son had got hold of the gas and the mob made its way to the police station, with Hamid my brother at its head: a procession of flaming torches snaked from the dump, chanting murderous threats, fulminating against "the Doberman." Luckily for him, the creep was somewhere else and escaped the

conflagration, which we danced round like demons
in a trance. Some boys threw stones or spat blasphe-
mies into the air, while others pulled out their dicks
and pissed at the flames; the spectacle was never to be
forgotten. The caretaker was spared, because he was a
local kid. All the same, he was stripped naked and his
uniform suspended from a stick, which we hoisted like
a macabre flag, uttering cries of victory before fling-
ing it on the fire. If he'd been there, "the Doberman"
would have been lynched. We'd have ripped his stink-
ing fat belly to shreds. We'd have smashed the jaw that
spewed such bullshit, releasing the aggression built up
over a decade. Still, the outcome was decisive, since we
never saw that bastard's sinister face again. Or, in fact,
any uniforms at all. The police station never got rebuilt and no one was too bothered. From then on, dif-
ferences between people were resolved either through
the elders' mediation or by a fistfight at the dump. And
by and large, life in Sidi Moumen picked up and carried on its own sweet way.

5

CONTRARY TO APPEARANCES, Ali was white. Like his coalman father, he couldn't get rid of the dark complexion that went with the job. He'd grown used to it, and to the nickname "Blackie" he'd been saddled with from a young age—unjustly, given that he was only intermittently black. On Fridays, when he left the hammam, he'd cover up his temporary natural color, which he found almost shameful, since many people didn't recognize him. Of all my friends, Ali was Yemma's favorite—and for good reason. He'd hardly ever come round empty-handed: he always had a small bag of coal he'd swipe from the shop, claiming it was a present from his father. Which was a lie as fat as a watermelon. Knowing Omar the coalman, it was unlikely that that skinflint would do anyone a favor. He spent his life cloistered in his little booth, his shoulder bag tucked under an unflinching arm, guarding his stash in the hollow of a damp, hot armpit. You scarcely knew he was there, so completely had he merged with the mountain of coal over which he reigned, a true king of the fire, as he was called. And don't imagine for a moment he'd add a little extra when it came to the weighing, as shopkeepers normally do. Omar monitored the balance of the scales as if he were selling gold nuggets. But people didn't hold it against him, and many found it funny. In any case, they didn't have much choice, since His Majesty was the only coal merchant in Sidi Moumen.

His son Ali was the bane of his life—a gaping wound he cursed morning and night. In his eyes, that spend-thrift was only out to squander the family assets and had no other interests besides squelching around in the mud behind a ball. And he never missed a chance to tell him so. Yet Ali didn't suffer too much because, in time, he'd become used to his father's bombast; he no longer even heard him grumbling or endlessly lamenting his fate. Ali would slave from dawn till dusk, in silence, lifting twenty-kilo sacks, bringing meals from home, washing the dishes, scrubbing down the shop front, and performing a whole series of backbreaking jobs. He'd barely stop for breath before he had to jump up for the next chore. His only moments of respite were at prayer times, when his father would go to the mosque: a good half hour, during which Ali hurriedly did his deals on the side, thus ensuring he had his daily pocket money. There were good days and bad days, but on average he'd get together about five dirhams, which earned him kudos in our group. Not counting my brother Hamid, he was the richest of us all. And the most generous, since his contribution to the team's coffers far outstripped ours. Omar the coalman's only means of controlling his son was to check the shopping of the people he passed in the street. If, unhappily, he spotted coal in someone's basket, he'd rush to check the books. At the least suspicion of theft, the situation took a dramatic turn: grabbing the braided ox's tail he used as a whip, he'd douse it in a bucket of water and crack it, ramping up the terror endured by Ali, who'd be crouching and shielding his face. He'd thrash him with all his might, until he drew blood. As a result, Ali would take serious precautions before doing any fiddling, making sure, for example, that a customer was going in the opposite direction from the mosque, or selling the coal half price to an accomplice. And if there'd been no customers while he was away, Omar would deliver a violent slap . . . just in case. Ali had adapted to this too, developing a surprising technique for evading slaps while seeming to take them: anticipating the hand's trajectory, he'd sink his neck between his shoulders at the crucial moment, letting out a yelp like a dog whose tail has been trodden on. Eventually, like many of us, he'd gotten used to these blows. Now they were part and parcel of his life—like the bitterness of humiliation, the ugliness that pressed in on us from all sides, and the cursed fate that had delivered us, bound hand and foot, to this nameless rubble.

When he came over to our place, Ali would insist Yemma let him light the fire. Like a real magician, he'd place an oil-soaked rag on top of a pyramid of coal and, in next to no time, the brazier was aflame. Yemma would sing his praises, telling me: "You should be more like your friend, look how talented he is!" Then she'd offer us mint tea and those biscuits made with salty butter that we loved so much. Though she could seem blunt, and sometimes obdurate, Yemma had a big heart. She seemed to be carrying all of Sidi Moumen's distress on her shoulders. Never one to refuse food to a hungry friend, she'd always find him a little something: a bit of bread soaked in puréed broad beans, a bowl of soup, a hard-boiled egg, or anything else she could lay her hands on.

Yemma showed Ali such tenderness I'd sometimes be jealous, especially when I caught her stroking his hair or whispering in his ear. Also, she'd mischievously call him Yussef, which was not his name. Ali's face would instantly turn crimson and he'd look down to hide his eyes, which were filled with tears. I'd watch the two of them stupidly, unable to make sense of their closeness. It was a long time before I discovered the secret of the painful story that made Yemma's heart bleed. She revealed it to me one morning to console me after Ali and I had argued. I'd come home annoyed, and had lain down on a mat, not saying a word. Sitting in the yard, her legs either side of a small table heaped with lentils she was sifting through, Yemma gave me a quick glance. That was enough for her to read my mood.

"Come here, my son, bring me your eyes, I can't see these damned stones anymore."

I sat down beside her and began picking over the lentils too.

"You look so sad, what's happened?"

"Nothing."

"Come on now, tell your old mother what's bothering you."

"It doesn't matter. I had a fight with Ali."

"Over nothing, I imagine!"

I kept quiet. Yemma paused before going on:

"Still, he's a good boy. He isn't bad."

Then, fixing her attention on the pulses, she said in a hushed voice, as if fearing she'd be overheard: "You should be kind to him. That boy hasn't had much luck."

I looked at her in astonishment.

"You know many round here who have?"

She smiled.

"But he's definitely had less luck than others. I'm going to tell you his story, but first you have to promise me you won't repeat it . . . even though it's no secret to anyone!"

"Well, it is to me."

"Your friend's name isn't really Ali."

"Well, I know that much, Yemma. We call him Blackie."

"Listen to me and stop interrupting. Your friend's birth name was Yussef. I know because I was there when he was baptized. I also know his poor mother, who I see at the hammam all the time. Ali is his brother's name."

"You're wrong, Yemma. He doesn't have a brother."

"That's true—not anymore. Ali was a lovely boy. I watched him grow, just as I have watched you."

"I don't understand."

"It's a tragic story, my son, one you wouldn't wish on your worst enemy."

She cleared her throat, let out a deep sigh, and went on: "There was a heat wave that summer, it was one of the hottest we've ever known. People couldn't stay indoors because the zinc roofs, conspiring with the sun, turned homes into blazing furnaces. It was no better outside. The chergui was blowing clouds of dust and dirt from the east, making it impossible to breathe. The sky was heavy and low and constantly red; the atmosphere was stifling, a feeling of apocalypse hovered over Sidi Moumen. Yussef had dragged his younger brother,

Ali, down to the river, below the quarries. It hadn't yet dried up in those days. Although it was contaminated by the town sewers, that river attracted a good many kids who'd pour in from faraway slums to cool off. It was a real beach, my son. I'd sometimes take your older brothers there. They'd run riot, swimming from morning till night. I'd make tuna and tomato sandwiches and we'd get there early. The trees weren't burnt by the sun and clouds of birds would come to tickle the green leaves. I loved seeing your father stretched out on the grass, his transistor radio glued to his ear, thrilling to the sports commentators' wild outbursts. He'd make me laugh because if a Widad player happened to score, he'd suddenly jerk to his feet like a goat and dance a manic jig, then he'd throw himself on top of me and squeeze me tight. I protested, of course: 'Magdul, what are you doing? People are watching!' But he paid no attention. He was like a kid . . ."

Yemma fell silent, she seemed to be in a dream. She'd forgotten her lentils and the story she was meant to be telling me. Her face glowed with light. I didn't make a sound, so as not to interrupt her reverie. I found it hard to imagine my father belonging to the world of the living, and Yemma a woman in love. After a while, she recovered herself.

"Your brother Hamid was uncontrollable, incorrigible, king of the mischief makers. That was why

I constantly kept my eye on the river. I'd catch him throwing himself off the bridge all the time. The water wasn't deep and there was every chance he'd hit his head on a rock. It was no good me shouting myself hoarse, or shaking my arms at him, he just ignored me. The little fiend did exactly as he pleased. Your father objected, telling me to let the boys be, but I couldn't stop worrying. Looking back on it, I don't think Yussef should have taken his little brother to the river. There was danger everywhere. Ali was just five and Yussef only slightly older. Omar the coalman's last-born was his pride and joy; he treated him like a prince, despite his miserly ways. He'd never come home at night without a little treat for him, chickpeas or sunflower seeds wrapped in newspaper. Inevitably, Yussef was jealous, but he loved his brother. He'd certainly have stopped him jumping off the bridge if he'd known he would disappear forever. It wasn't fair of Omar the coalman to call him a murderer. So many little kids flung themselves haphazardly off the bridge. I saw them with my own eyes. They'd resurface a little farther down, unharmed. But not Ali, the little devil. Keen to show how brave he was, he raced to hurl himself off first, with a roar. And then he didn't come back up. The river had just sucked up his shouts and his childish laughter. Forever. And yet the water wasn't deep. Maybe a little rough that day, but Ali could swim. It wasn't the first time he'd followed his brother to the river. How could Omar the coalman, having just lost one son, annihilate the other with such lethal words? 'Murderer!' he shouted, to anyone who'd listen. The many witnesses spoke of an accident, not a crime. A rock must have shattered the little one's skull and the current took care of the rest. At first Yussef thought it was a joke; Ali used to delight in scaring him. Then, with fear in his gut, a frenzied fear he'd never known before, he threw himself in too. He looked for his brother everywhere. Wide-eyed, he dived down into the cloudy water and dived again. Nothing. He stayed submerged in the water for hours, frozen and trembling. The little body had disappeared, as if swallowed by the shifting clay; the hungry, malicious clay had devoured the laughing little boy. Some local shepherds set to work, raking the river from bank to bank. The boy was nowhere to be found, it was as if he'd vanished. It took the men of Sidi Moumen several days before they fished out the corpse a mile away from the scene. It was not a pretty sight, he was all decomposed; *a fistful of mud*, his mother moaned, rolling herself in the dust, scratching and tearing at her face. 'Give me back my mud,' she murmured, in a voice that gave you goose bumps. As for Yussef, he ran away, disappearing for a whole week because he knew how violent his father could be. He trailed around near Chichane and Toma, unable to face the fury that he knew was unavoidable. In fact, he'd almost been forgotten, the grief-stricken household was in complete disarray, with people filing in and out from morning till night. If the imam had not intervened, his disappearance might have lasted for eternity. It was the imam, a man respected by everyone, who went to fetch Yussef from the other side of the dump, promising him his father would be merciful, and who made the coalman swear, with his hand on the Koran, to spare his son the punishment he felt he deserved a thousand times over . . ."

My mother broke off; sobs were blocking her throat. I too felt like crying but I stopped myself.

"Tell me, Yemma, why did Yussef change his name?"

My mother wiped her nose on the edge of her gandoura and went on: "One evening, after the burial, Omar the coalman summoned his wife and children into a room and said, in a voice that might have sounded sweet had it not dripped with hate: 'I promised the imam I would not slash this criminal's throat. Not that I don't want to, but I will keep my promise. From this day on, know that it is not Ali who is dead, it's Yussef, his murderer. He is dead and buried. I never want to hear his name again. He does not exist. He has never existed. If any one of you makes even the slightest reference to him, you will be turned out of my house. Do you understand me?' They all looked down.

Then, turning to Yussef, who was cowering, petrified, in a corner, he said firmly: 'From now on, your name is Ali. This way, your crime will follow you to hell.' More serious still, in his statement to the police, the coalman gave Yussef as the name of the drowned child." My mother sighed. "And that is how the friend you're so angry with right now officially lost his identity."

That distressing story stayed with me for a very long time. On so many occasions I almost called Blackie by his real name, but I stopped myself. In the end, his nickname sorted things out: it saved us from punishing him forever. Yet, many years later, coming out of the garage, we'd gathered at the bus stop on our way to the city. Half the Stars of Sidi Moumen were there, divided into two groups. Blackie was in the second group. The sun blazed down on the peach-colored ramparts. The birds were chirping as if nothing was wrong. Cars came and went, trailing clouds of black exhaust fumes. A few donkeys with hollow bellies strained to haul their ramshackle carts, piled high with all sorts of junk. Cyclists panted up the hill. Just the ordinary hubbub of an ordinary day. Behind us sprawled Sidi Moumen and its garbage trucks, its dump and its poor. What we were thinking at that moment, I couldn't say. Probably nothing. We were wearing our paradise belts around our thudding hearts, awaiting deliverance. Ali and I hugged each other for a long time and said those words that even today resonate strangely in my mind:

"See you up there, Yachine."

"Yes, Yussef, see you up there."

It was the first time I'd called him by his real name. He smiled at me and gave a shrug of resignation.

Our group caught the first bus.

6

IN SOCCER, DEFENDING players have lower status than attacking players. People only ever remember the goal scorers. And yet, the real battle is fought at the back and in midfield. If Khalil, our central defender, didn't command attention, he was very much a linchpin of the team. And I have to admit, I owe a good part of my notoriety to him. Without good defenders, a goalkeeper is lost; he lets everything in. In fact, I'd like to pay public tribute to that talented boy. There, it's done. The truth is, Khalil and I didn't have much in common. We'd always be bickering on the field. And sometimes off it, too. One day, accusing me of siding with the enemy, because of a save I'd missed, he threw a broken bottle at me, without warning, which cut me on the left shoulder. It was no big deal, just a scratch, but at the sight of blood, my brother came charging over, right in the middle of the game, swinging his bicycle chain, and laid into him with insane violence, almost finishing him off. I remember a curious thing: Khalil, barely conscious, scrabbling in the dust, trying to locate the two teeth he'd just lost, as if he could stick them back in, like a bridge he could simply replace to restore his smile. Hamid, whose strength increased tenfold at times like this, was bellowing like a wild animal as he went at him. The others hadn't attempted to separate them because no one liked this stuck-up boy who'd just turned up from the city and thought the sun shone out of his ass. Forming a circle round the brawl, stoking the rage in my brother's eyes, they were yelling in unison: "Kill him! Kill him!" Curled up on the ground, his hands protecting his bruised face, Khalil begged us for help, calling on the good Lord and His saints. But the good Lord wasn't around; He'd long since turned His august gaze away from Sidi Moumen. I fought like the devil to extract my brother from the scrum and got punched in the process, which hurt a lot more than the scratch that had started the fight. Restraining Hamid once he'd lost it was some feat. He broke free and let rip again, giving his victim an extra pummeling. The players were thrilled; they clapped as if they were celebrating a victory. One of them seized the chance to land a kick on the poor kid, who'd finally lost consciousness. That encouraged the rest of them and it turned into a real lynching. When my brother had calmed down, the injured boy was evacuated to the sideline and the game resumed as if nothing had happened.

Tall and thin, as ugly as hell (and losing his teeth didn't help matters), Khalil always looked down on us. The fact that his family had tumbled from the city to the slums made him superior to us: he hadn't been born poor—or at least so he claimed. In any case, he never missed an opportunity to brag about it. And yet he had to be unhappier than most of the local low-lifes. Being born in squalor is more bearable than being shoved into it later on. And even if he exaggerated his cosseted past, there was no doubt he'd come down in the world. The seediest alleyways of the medina are a lot better than our shantytown.

The son of a coach driver, with three younger sisters, Khalil might have avoided Sidi Moumen if a terrible accident hadn't turned their lives upside down. The only horse his family possessed broke its leg, setting off a series of events that threw them on the scrap heap. After the animal had been put down, there was only one way to buy another: selling their house. The decision was a difficult one. Leaving the home of their forefathers was unthinkable. Their father wavered for a long time, asking advice from his closest friends, turning the question over in his mind a hundred times before he took the plunge and sold his property to a returning emigrant who'd just arrived from a Paris suburb and paid cash. Their mother sobbed as she followed the removal cart her husband had borrowed, loaded with all their possessions. Khalil didn't understand what was happening. He was quite happy sitting among the furniture as the little cart made its way down the congested alleyways. First they went to live with an uncle, just until they sorted themselves out financially. But an argument between his mother and his aunt forced them out again. A long year at the home of his grandfather, who was himself already crammed into a confined space with several other families, and then they ran aground in Sidi Moumen, where all downward slides converge. In the meantime, instead of buying another horse and going back to his old job, the coach driver decided, in a move he considered shrewd, to invest his savings in a Chinese prescription-glasses business, which proved to be a disaster. And, since forgery was involved, in addition to having his merchandise confiscated, he could have gone to prison. The remainder of his money wound up in the pocket of the judge, who spared him that fate. As for the con man—that charming crook who claimed he'd knocked about a bit in the business world and had promised them the earth—he vanished into thin air, leaving the coach driver and his family in the gutter, on their knees. It took them a long time to get back up again, but the father still had some fight left. With the help of a few friends, he built adobe walls at the end of a row of shacks, covering them with a roof of corrugated iron, plastic, branches, and stones. He dismantled his now useless coach and could at least chop up the wood to make doors and windows. Then he went into selling single cigarettes.

The miracle of Sidi Moumen is the strange facility with which new arrivals adapt. Coming from parched fields or voracious metropolises, driven out by blind authority and the parasitical rich, they slip into the mold of resigned defeat, grow used to the filth, throw their dignity to the winds, learn to get by, to patch up their lives. As soon as they've made their nest, they sink into it, they go to ground, and it's as if they've always been there and have never done anything but add to the surrounding poverty. They become part of the landscape, like the mountain of sewage, like the make-shift shelters, built of mud and spit, topped by satellite dishes like gigantic upturned ears. They're here and they dream. They know the grim reaper is lurking, and that those who've given up dreaming will be first to go. But they are not going to die. They stick together; they support each other. Disease lies in wait, they can see it, can smell it. They defy it. Hunger may well stretch out its tentacles, gripping throats till they choke, but in Sidi Moumen it does not kill, because people share what little they have. Because they look to each other to measure their common distress. Tomorrow, it will be so-and-so's turn. The day after, someone else's. The wheel turns so fast. Between little and nothing lie a few crumbs, blown away by the merest breath.

The coach driver married off his two elder daughters to the first comers. Fewer mouths to feed is always a good thing. For big celebrations a ceremonial tent is erected near the pump. The ground is covered with carpets borrowed from neighbors, drapes are hung and decorated with palm leaves, dozens of lanterns are dotted around the place, and, for as long as the party lasts, the guests, all dressed up, imagine they're living on the other side of the wall. The coach driver did not disappoint: he bled himself dry to give his daughters proper weddings, calling on Tamu each time to make a real night of it.

Khalil left school and became a shoeshine boy, working the streets, cafés, and all the bustling city squares.

Little by little, he became part of our group. He toned down his arrogance, and we became more easygoing, less aggressive. He'd often join us in the evenings at Nabil's shack. He'd bring a bottle of Coca-Cola and some Henry's cookies or a bit of hash, with his American tobacco and rolling papers. He'd tell us all about his fabulous days in the medina, his struggle for control of a strategic square, the tricks he'd use to deceive the café waiters, who'd chase off all interlopers: kids renting out newspapers, pedlars of contraband, pimps, pickpockets, shoeshine boys . . . He'd describe to us in great detail the exquisite meals he'd treat himself to if the morning was successful: spicy sausage sandwich, puréed broad beans with olive oil and cumin, calves' feet or a sheep's head, roasted to perfection. He'd make our mouths water with all these marvels. On Fridays, he'd say, people give away couscous and whey outside their front doors. He'd been known to devour three breakfasts in a row, elbowing beggars out of the way to grab a bit of meat.

We knew he was exaggerating, but we loved hearing it anyway. He said it was a shame that slippers don't need polishing, otherwise he'd have made a fortune! But he couldn't complain. His father had set him a reasonable sum to bring home at the end of the day. And he managed it. And not by taking the easy way out like other boys his age: he only rarely had sex with tourists, even though it brought in the equivalent of a day's work. No, that wasn't his style, or only at times of extreme hardship.

And that was how, on account of a wretched broken leg, a family's destiny had darkened. Though Khalil and I buried the hatchet, it was only years later that we spent any time together, at the garage. And that was because of Abu Zoubeir.

7

WITH BOYS LIKE Khalil the shoeshine, Nabil, the son of Tamu, Ali (or Yussef), alias Blackie, Fuad, and my brother Hamid, we made up our own little family; it was us against the world. If any of us was in trouble, the others would rise up as one to rescue him. When Fuad, for example, started sniffing glue, we waged a ruthless campaign to get him off it. But he carried on in secret. So many times I'd find him standing at his stall, completely out of it, letting little kids pinch his cakes, not pelting them with stones like he normally would. Worse, the brats were shameless enough to pick his pockets, as if he were a no-good drunk. Fuad was gone. He was traveling in his head. I could shake him all I liked, he wouldn't respond. His eyes, wide open, were contemplating a world I had no access to. So I just picked up whatever was left of his cakes and dragged him back home. As soon as his mother opened the door, she'd explode in a torrent of threats and abuse. We'd be lucky if she let us in at all. I'd carry my friend into a room the size of a storage cupboard and put him down on a mat like a bundle. He just let me do it. Sometimes, he'd smile at me, a sign he was still alive.

When Fuad lost his father, his uncle Mbark (now the muezzin) married his mother—in order, they claimed, to save the children from an outsider's clutches. It was an old custom, which Fuad never managed to accept, especially as it meant losing his position as head of the family. I think his addiction to glue began in reaction to this marriage—which is unnatural, whatever they say. Fuad was incapable of smoking kif or hashish like everyone else. The smallest toke would set off a coughing fit that had him doubled up on the ground. Glue suited him better; it was his only means of escape. We tried excluding him from the group for a long time, but we didn't give up on him. Obviously, we couldn't do without his skills on the field, but he was no longer welcome at Nabil's. One important detail: he never sniffed glue on Sundays, game days, as if soccer gave him more of a high than the junk he was constantly inhaling. My brother Hamid's hard-line stance paid off in the end; Fuad suffered greatly from the isolation. He'd reacted angrily at first, threatening to leave the Stars and play for a rival team, but in the end he gave in. It was around that time that he and his sister, Ghizlane, moved in with their grandmother in Douar Scouila. One day, in front of everyone, he gave his black, sticky handkerchief and his tubes of glue to another addict who happened to be walking past. It was over. He never touched the stuff again.

Over time, we did up Nabil's shack, putting in benches, a carpet, a round trestle table, and lots of pouffes. If the radio-cassette player broke (and it often did), we'd make the music ourselves with all kinds of percussion instruments: tam-tams, darbukas, saucepans. Sometimes Nabil would let loose, launching into a performance in imitation of his mother. He had a beautiful voice. He'd make us laugh so much when he stood up to dance. He'd shake his ass in perfect time to the music, undulating his shoulders, making his head move sideways, as if each part of his body was detached from the rest. As if his limbs were obeying different brains, conducted with brio by an angel with an invisible baton. He had such white skin, Nabil, and his wavy, chestnut-brown hair had a strange effect on us. Hamid couldn't resist taunting him, calling him by his mother's name: Tamu this, Tamu that. Nabil would laugh along with us, but he didn't stop dancing. He was swept up by a secret, powerful, heavy swell, sculpting the cloud of smoke that got thicker and thicker, itself describing a thousand arabesques. Spliffs passed from hand to hand, the songs grew louder. I remember one night seeing the corrugated iron roof lift off, inviting the infinite sky to join the party. I saw stars, the moon, and red bats' eyes winking at me.

I also remember (and how deeply I regret it) the shameful episode that shattered our new family. It was in August, at the height of the blistering heat. We'd just won a crucial game against the Serpents of Douar Lahjar, our long-standing rivals. Fuad had played brilliantly, scoring so many goals that it was looking like a complete massacre. Khalil, our central defender, had put his mantra into practice: striker gets past without ball, ball gets past without striker, never both together. His bravado cost him quite a few injuries and a black eye. And I don't want to brag, but I was on fire, leaping like Yachine in his glory days. Gravity couldn't touch my elastic body. The only goal I'd let in, everyone agreed, was unstoppable. So, rejoicing in our crushing victory, we decided to celebrate that night at Nabil's. Everyone had brought something. Khalil had tracked down some first-class hash—it was greenish, almost black, and gorgeously sticky. We rolled and smoked joint after joint, sipping coffee mixed with nutmeg. Hamid had made us an explosive concoction, Coca-Cola with a slug of methylated spirits, which blew our heads off. Intoxicated by our triumph and the meths, we sang and danced, first alone, then in each other's arms. Nabil was euphoric. He'd put on a white gandoura, knotted a belt round his thighs to emphasize the gyrating of his hips, and had taken the floor, a circle forming round him. The radio-cassette player worked like a dream. The percussion reverberated all around us, inside us, making the blood rush in our veins, making it pulsate; our ordinarily anemic faces were flushed with the exhilaration of great feasts, of gris-gris and marabouts in wild trances. This world we'd entered was unreal, far from all the filth and the dross, from hunger and its ghosts. The only thing that mattered was the overpowering feeling of invincibility that flooded us. We were kings, on top of the world, blind drunk, swimming in the clouds, clapping our hands and screaming for joy. Nabil's gandoura ballooned around him as he whirled. He fluttered his eyelashes and spun round and round, pirouetting endlessly. Then, like a parachutist surrounded by his silk, he collapsed on the floor, in a faint. You could have sworn an amorous, jealous angel had conspired to make him fall. I don't know what came over my brother, but he swooped on him like a vulture. Hamid always took his adversaries by surprise; that was his trademark. He'd strike the moment their guard was lowered. But now he started kissing Nabil, who did not react but lay there inert, as if dead. The countless glasses of alcohol we'd downed in the course of the evening had a lot to do with it. Hamid kissed him, or rather devoured him with kisses, as if he'd always desired him and was now finally able to take his revenge, throw off his inhibitions and ferociously trample his frustration. Then, pausing momentarily, he surveyed the excited horde, and, un-embarrassed by our presence, he calmly stripped Nabil, pulled out his own cock, which was stiff as a rod, and planted it in the plump, pinkish, exposed rump. He did it so straightforwardly it was unnerving. It didn't seem to shock anyone, apart from me. Whatever Hamid did he did quickly, and the sex act didn't last long. I'd turned round so as not to see the grim spectacle; I could only hear moaning, mingled with the singing of Nass El Ghi-wane. Then it was Fuad's turn to straddle the sleeping boy. He did so delicately, nuzzling and stroking his mount as if they were setting off on a long journey. Nabil was un-conscious, laid out in the middle of the room like a corpse. Fuad sat astride him, whispering unintelligible words in his ear. A squawk like a bird's, then a yelp, like someone being stabbed. And on to the next. Ali made a show of remorse, hesitating briefly, and finally took the plunge. Khalil was not to be outdone. He was raring to go, grum-bling that the dark-skinned boy was taking his time. He pushed Ali off, unsheathed his prick and went at it. His groans made the whole room erupt with laughter. There was only me left. I don't know why I didn't listen to my heart, which ordered me to leave, to run away as fast as I could from this accursed, hellish place. I stayed where I was, head down, stuck in a nightmare from which there was no escape. I felt their challenging stares forcing me into a corner, my back against the wall. I was rooted to the spot, I didn't know which way to turn. Hamid had left the room so as not to witness my shame. He knew my frailties, my cowardice. As God is my witness, I tried to step up. I had to prove to them I wasn't a wimp, I was no queer. My honor—or my ass—was at stake. I went over to Nabil, trembling, thinking I could manage it, if only my lifeless dick showed some interest. Beads of sweat trickled slowly down my forehead, taking the route of tears and falling onto the naked body right in front of me. There were tears mixed with my sweat for sure; I recognized their salty taste in my mouth. At that precise moment, Nabil opened his eyes—eyes that were pitiful, bewildered, bereft. He must have been wondering what was happening. Had he committed a foul in the game that he was paying for now? Had he hurt someone? He didn't know. Nor did I. In any case, his gaze banished any heroics my friends were expecting of me. They weren't holding it against me, anyway, because I watched them slink off one after the other, as if they'd abruptly sobered up, suddenly realizing the depravity of their act. I stayed by Nabil's mortified body for a long time, in silence. He struggled to get the words out: "So what happened?"

I did not reply. I just pulled his gandoura down over his nakedness, over his disarray and humiliation, the way a stage curtain is lowered at the end of a macabre play.

8

IT WASN'T ALL violence in Sidi Moumen. What I'm giving you is a condensed version of eighteen years on a swarming anthill, so obviously it's a bit turbulent. These sorry episodes leave their mark on a young life. And a young death, too. A death almost without a corpse, because they had to scrape mine off the ground bit by bit. Ironically, they buried Khalil's remains in with me: a jawbone with teeth missing, two fingers of a right hand, the one that had set off the device, and a foot with its ankle, because we'd had the bright idea of buying identical espadrilles. The burial was a rush job, because clearly he had bigger feet than me. So here we are, resting side by side in the same plot in the shadow of a jujube tree at the back of the cemetery—two boys who never got on. We weren't entitled to any prayers because no one prays at the graves of suicides.

I can still see my father, my brothers, and the most
fearless of the Stars of Sidi Moumen standing round
the hole I'd just been lowered into. I say fearless because they knew they wouldn't escape a second sum-
mons to police headquarters. And our police aren't
famous for their compassion. When they nab a suspect
somewhere, his whole village gets pulled in. But they
wanted to be there. My father, who'd long claimed he
couldn't walk, had followed the pitiful procession on
foot. And didn't budge till the last spadeful. It was as if
he'd picked up a few scraps of the life I'd just lost. My
older brothers stood next to him, watchful in case his
legs gave way. But Father stood firm, his chest thrust
out like a soldier's, barely leaning on the knob of his
cane. He was the first to notice Yemma walk in. Yemma, or what remained of her.

She'd left home the day the police armada invaded
our shack and turned the place upside down. She'd
been informed of the carnage I, my brother Hamid,
and other terrorists had wreaked in the city: the dozens of innocent victims, the massive material damage,
the entire country's panic. Yemma, in the yard, had
crumpled over an upturned basin, and took refuge in a
strange silence. She merely observed the commotion as
if it had nothing to do with her, as if the children who'd
just died were not hers. She did not weep, she did not
groan. The nest she'd built over so many years, with

such care, suddenly swept off in a whirlwind, belonged
to some other woman. No, it wasn't her husband, or
her remaining children, that the police were unceremo-
niously marching off in handcuffs. This was a gang of
strangers roughing up other strangers, amid sounds of
screams and pleading, as often happened in the slum.
Nor did she see her neighbors, who came en masse to
comfort her. She didn't hear their siren wails, nor did
she feel their repeated, insistent embraces. She watched
people and things with the same lethargy that would
come over her in the evenings, in front of the television,
when she managed to make us watch an Egyptian soap
opera. We'd wait for her to doze off before changing the
channel; she was always so tired she'd be asleep within
five minutes. But she wasn't sleeping now. Taking advantage of the confusion, she simply stood up and left,
not bothering to put on her djellaba, or even her slippers. No one saw her again, until the day of our burial.
My brothers searched for her everywhere, mobilizing
the entire family. They began with the nearby slums:
Chichane, Toma, Douar Lahjar, Douar Scouila; then
they went inside the city walls, combing the farthest
alleyways of the medina. They hammered on the doors
of mosques and holy men, in case she had melted into
the magma of beggars. But no, she had vanished. The
police were looking for her too, for further question-
ing. And God knows, every square inch of that city was

patrolled by as many representatives of law and order as the country could possibly muster.

And now, suddenly, here she was, as if by a miracle. This creature, all in rags, with disheveled hair, walking barefoot along the path overgrown with thistles, staring into space in the middle of the cemetery, was indeed my beloved mother. She had come to say her goodbyes. A hubbub of protest broke out, since women are not admitted to the cemetery on burial days. Yemma paid no attention; she advanced slowly, like a tightrope walker on a wire, one foot in front of the other. She would not falter now that she was so close to her goal. My brothers' impulse was to rush over to her, but Father stopped them in their tracks. The silence grew even heavier than it had been at any moment of that torrid day in that accursed month of May. The crowd gathered around my grave parted to let her through. Scores of eyes stared at the sickly creature who, as naturally as could be, was defying an immutable tradition. She came right up to the edge, as if she might throw herself in and lie down by my side, as if she might let out the sobs her throat had held back for so long. But she did not. She simply muttered a jumbled verse from the Koran, alone at first, the grave diggers looking on aghast, then accompanied by a blind beggar, whose hoarse voice sent shivers down everyone's spine. My father too began to chant, then my brothers, and finally everyone else. The rest of the beggars, who until then had been standing at a distance, now joined the group, breaking into a shrill dirge, the better to earn the dried figs and dates they were expecting. But there was no woman at home to think about alms or funeral customs, or to greet people coming to offer their condolences. That said, there wasn't exactly a crowd of them, because plainclothes police were constantly on the prowl. Every passerby was a potential terrorist. So people hid indoors and hardly went out. The dump, too, was deserted, completely lifeless. No one was sifting through the rubbish the trucks went on tipping. There was not a single kid's shout. Only the astonished birds and cats, left in peace, scavenged to their hearts' content. A morose mood hung over Sidi Moumen, like the one that now pervaded the desolate cemetery where we'd played so often as kids. We'd come to torment the drunks who sought sanctuary there. We'd throw stones at them and run off, squealing. They were in such a bad way they could never catch us. As they tried to give chase, my brother Hamid would double back and nick their bundles. We'd be helpless with laughter, especially when he set fire to them and danced round the blaze . . .

The gravediggers carried on with their work in an atmosphere that was almost normal. They placed flat stones over my remains, as if to stop me from escaping the realm of shadows, and covered me with earth, which they packed down, pouring liters of orange blossom water on top. So it was that this slip of a woman, whom some thought mad, managed to impose on the men a burial that was worthy of her sons.

"Where's Hamid?" Yemma demanded, addressing my father. He glanced toward a nearby grave that had been freshly filled in. She went over and crouched down beside it. Hamid was the rebel of the family, but, between you and me, he was her favorite. Even though she shouted at him all day long for his never-ending mischief, and whipped him whenever he went too far, the fact remained that she loved him more than the rest of us, because she and he were alike. They were cut from the same cloth, businesslike in everything they undertook. If she wanted something done right, Yemma entrusted it to Hamid and to Hamid alone. He'd always make good, he never came back empty-handed. His entrepreneurial spirit filled her with pride. And though she disapproved of the way he made his money, she was always pleased to see him dressed like the rich kids, in blue jeans and the latest trainers, with his slicked-back hair—which she thought looked greasy and sticky, even though she accepted that it was the fashion. She'd also turn a blind eye when he took me to the tailor's to get me fitted for a waistcoat or saroual, or brought hazelnut chocolates for Father. Sometimes he'd give her perfume, which she accepted, protesting. She'd immediately put it away in her wardrobe, which she'd double-lock, and take it out again on feast days. Yemma loved the sweet fragrances in those pretty bottles the smugglers brought from Ceuta. If I surprised her putting some on, she'd dab a drop behind my ears and give me a kiss. Now, though, she was in no mood for celebration and didn't smell of Hamid's musky perfume. Squatting in front of this heap of damp earth, her hands covered her lined face, where wrinkles, feeding on grief, had spun their webs in no time at all. Yemma's eyes had almost disappeared, as if they'd been swallowed by her eyelids. They'd lost their sparkle; they were just two insignificant little holes. In the old days, those eyes could make us tremble. Yemma had only to look at one of us to hypnotize us. Now her eyes were dead, just like Hamid and me, like Khalil, Nabil, Ali: dead because of the people we'd met at the garage, "the emir and his companions," as Abu Zoubeir called them. Well, I'll tell you more about those guys later. There were four of them, come from the neighboring slums to guide us back to the straight and narrow. They knew the Koran by heart, as well as the sayings of the Prophet, as if they'd formed part of his entourage. That made us feel inferior. Abu Zoubeir said we could learn them too if we just put our minds to it. Anyone could learn.

The crowd moved from my grave to my brother's. People formed a circle round my mother, her dead child at her feet. The grave was already filled in, but Yemma moved her hands over the damp soil as if Hamid might still feel her caress. She leaned over to kiss the earth and her face was all streaked with dirt. Said, our eldest brother, took a handkerchief from his pocket, wiped her face, and sat down beside her. As she didn't object, he edged his arm round her shoulders and pulled her toward him. Little by little she softened. My other brothers joined them. Scenting a tip, the blind beggar followed up with a sura from the Koran that told of the gates to paradise, open wide to the deceased, and the blessings that awaited him there: rivers of milk, wine, and honey; the virgin houris, eternally beautiful young men, and other marvels. He recited with such conviction that he almost made you want to stretch out next to the dead boy. The other beggars upped their game. And Hamid, too, was permitted an almost normal burial.

When Said helped Yemma to her feet and put his arms round her, she let him do it. She seemed so light. He stroked her hair and pressed her to his chest. He whispered something in her ear that spread a shiver of light over her mournful face. It wasn't, strictly speaking, a smile, but the glow that usually lies behind it. He slid her onto his back and carried her home as if she were a sleeping child.

9

NO, IT WASN'T all darkness in Sidi Moumen. I had my
share of happiness too. My love affair with Ghizlane,
Fuad's younger sister, is proof of that. If there was one
thing for which I'd have given up the whole idea of leaving, it was my love for Ghizlane. To think so many lives
would have been spared if she'd held me back. Mine
for a start, and other people's—people I didn't know,
whom I carried off in my game bag like a poacher. I
know she'd have stopped me going beyond the point
of no return if only she'd taken me seriously. One night
we met up outside her grandmother's house. We'd often meet in that blind alley where few people ventured.
I tried to talk to her, hinting that it might be the last
time we'd see each other. She laughed in my face sar-
castically: "Watch you don't fall in the cesspools, they're
crawling with snakes and scorpions!" I knew every nook

and cranny of Sidi Moumen, all the mounds of fresh or recently scavenged rubbish, down to the last square inch of muck; so if I was going to fall in a ditch, it would be because I'd been pushed. It was no good my trying to look stern and serious or explaining it to her, she just kept laughing. Ghizlane was the funniest, liveliest, most radiant girl I ever had the good fortune to meet. The least thing would set her off. She'd slap her knees, and her whole body was so eloquent, you'd never notice how tiny she was. Her presence was so cheering it was as if garlands had been hung all round her, the kind used to decorate the wall on the Feast of the Throne. Her hazel eyes always sparkled, lighting up her face and its oval mouth with an irresistible mixture of charm and innocence. Despite her exuberance, and her slightly affected manner, she was sensitive and deep. When I was alive, I wouldn't have been able to describe her as I can now. I wasn't taught the words to convey the beauty of people or things, the sensuality and harmony that make them so glorious. And now, as a lovelorn ghost, I feel the futile need to pour out my feelings and finally tell this story I've been turning over and over in my mind since the day of my death.

In the beginning was the dump, teeming with its colony of rascals. The cult of soccer; the incessant fighting; the shoplifting and frantic getaways; the ups and downs of trying to survive; hashish, glue, and the strange places they took you; the black market and the small-time jobs; the repeated beatings; the sudden attempts at escape and their ransoms of rape and abuse . . . In the midst of all this chaos a glittering jewel had fallen from paradise: Ghizlane, my sweet and beautiful friend. No one knows how she landed in Sidi Moumen, but she was out of place in our filthy universe, a happy accident. I can still see her in the middle of her carrying hoop, a medium-sized rubber bucket on each side, going back and forth between the street pump and their home. In her long dress with wet patches, she seemed to glide over the loose stones and thistles on the path. The angel of grace had chosen this frail creature to blossom and live among us. If I wasn't helping Nabil at the dump, I'd offer to lend her a hand. She'd gladly accept and the mere sight of her white teeth made my heart quiver. We chatted as we walked. I'd sometimes do that journey several times in one morning, just as happily each time. I'd put up with my friends ribbing me, calling me a sissy, and with Hamid's jeers, if he happened to pass by. I loved being with her. Near the pump, we'd play at splashing each other, letting ourselves get soaked to the skin. We'd soon dry off in any case; Yemma would never notice a thing when I got home. Sometimes we'd stop near an isolated hut where, scorning the drought, a vine had clambered through the corrugated roof and reappeared through what must have once been windows. It was a shady place that, miraculously, no one had yet reclaimed. We secretly dreamed of living there one day, but we were too young to contemplate that kind of adventure.

Ghizlane would tell me about the dreadful atmosphere at home since the death of her father, the muezzin, and the marriage of her mother to Uncle Mbark. She didn't like that man, that hermit crab, who'd taken her father's place, taken over his job, his bed, his whole life. She didn't understand how her mother had metamorphosed into a harridan, one of those wicked witches straight out of fairy tales. True, Halima had never been the maternal type, but to neglect her own children to that extent verged on insanity. Now she had eyes only for her new husband, who'd become her lord and master; this man who'd turned her head, for whom she was willing to abandon everything. Was this recent or had it predated her husband's demise? No one could say. Whatever the truth of it, she'd spend hours making herself beautiful for him. It was as if she'd erased twenty years of her life to become the young, coquettish girl of the past again. Before sunset, she'd settle herself on cushions in the yard and bring out her beauty paraphernalia: a tiny round mirror and a case containing all kinds of powders, creams, and unguents. She attempted to brighten her eyes with a thick line of kohl, dragged almost to the ears, and enhance the coming kisses with lipstick from Fez, then she'd put on a delicately embroidered kaftan and sit herself on a kilim, like a young fiancée awaiting her suitor. When Mbark arrived, absinthe tea and dried fruits were produced, fresh candles were lit, and the transistor radio switched to the national channel, which broadcast popular tunes, patriotic songs to glorify the king, and official news bulletins. She hurried to bring him a basin of warm water with cooking salt for his foot massage. Soon after the radio soap opera, which the lovebirds wouldn't miss for anything in the world, Ghizlane would serve them supper, which they took à deux in their own room.

This was during the worst of Fuad's glue addiction, when he almost never came home, or if he did he was in a terrible state, his eyes rolled upward, red as two drops of blood. Ghizlane and I had made it our all but impossible mission to save him; she'd look after him indoors and outside it was up to me. She made him eat, wash, and change his clothes and would physically intervene when her mother, armed with a broad belt, came to give him a thrashing. "You're no longer part of this family!" Halima would say, summoning their uncle, who'd back her up with a verse from the Koran. Then she began to shriek: "That drug addict is driving me mad! What have I done to the good Lord to deserve such punishment?" Fuad was so far gone, he didn't even shield his face from the flailing blows.

Ghizlane caught a few in the cross fire, but still she put herself between them, defying her mother. Sometimes clumps of her hair were pulled out and she wouldn't make a sound. She'd get scratched, too, but she stood firm and waited for her mother to calm down before taking care of her brother, who'd be stretched out like a corpse on the palm mat. She took off his plastic sandals, slid a cushion under his head, and covered him with a blanket. She lay down next to him for a little while, to warm him up and comfort him, as her mother would have done had she not lost her mind.

Ghizlane's life was no fun—far from it. She didn't have any time to herself, she'd slave away all day long. She left the kitchen only to do the shopping, take the bread to the ovens, or fetch water from the pump. She'd make the meals, serve them, do the washing up, mop the cement section of the floor and sprinkle the rest. The afternoon was given over to laundry. She'd have to hang the washing on a line outside the house and, since they didn't have a terrace, she'd sit on a stool all afternoon to guard it, not just from thieves but in case the wind got up; then she had to take it down in a hurry, otherwise the clouds of dust would mean she had to start all over again. Meanwhile her mother, who'd taken early retirement, spent her days sipping tea with the neighbors, hanging around the souk as soon as a consignment of contraband was rumored to be arriving, or

keeping company with her oaf of a husband at meal-
times. The only contact she had with her daughter consisted of criticism and abuse, and usually ended in tears.
Life might have gone on this way if Ghizlane hadn't rebelled. And I played a part in it too. Together we worked
out a clever counterattack, an unexpected strategy from
a couple of twelve-year-olds. The plan was for Ghizlane
to fall asleep on the job and make a mess of anything she
possibly could: add too much salt to the tagines, leave it
out of the bread dough altogether, put a pinch of killer
chilli in salads, sweep before damping down the floor
so that dust spread right through the shack, leave stains
in the laundry or make new ones . . . in short, as far
as possible try to poison the sweet, peaceful life of her
stepfather and her hag of a mother. In spite of the hell
Ghizlane and Fuad were forced to endure for weeks on
end, the plan paid off. They put up with the beatings,
the humiliation and bullying. They were made to eat
those revolting meals, the salads that were on fire with
chilli, the gut-wrenching soups, while their mother and
Uncle Mbark brought delicious sandwiches back from
the market and shut themselves up in their room to eat
them. This war of attrition might have gone on indefi-
nitely had it not been for the intervention of Mi-Lalla,
their paternal grandmother. Heaven had sent her to put
an end to this situation, now become unbearable. She
suggested to Halima and Uncle Mbark that the children

come to stay with her until things settled down, explaining that it was normal for them to be upset by their father's death, their mother's remarrying so soon, and all the rest. A few weeks at most and things would be back to normal. Mother and uncle were only too willing, and it was salvation for all concerned. Ghizlane and Fuad packed their bags the same night and went to live with Mi-Lalla in Douar Scouila, a shantytown half an hour's walk from ours.

The Stars of Sidi Moumen took the news badly, fearing Fuad would be tempted away by his new neighborhood's local team. But that didn't happen. Moreover, a little while later, he stopped sniffing glue and was back to his dazzling best as our center forward. A new life was beginning for Ghizlane, too, since Mi-Lalla had taken her under her wing. She banned her from setting foot in the kitchen and enrolled her in an embroidery school run by someone she knew. "You have to have a trade, child, it's the only way to be free." Free: there was a word that resonated in Ghizlane's ears. It struck a chord, it consoled her. Yes, she would learn a trade and be free, vindicating the faith placed in her. She realized how lucky she was to have a grandmother like Mi-Lalla, who treated her so kindly, who fussed over her and spoke to her gently, who gave her the gold ring she'd been given by her own mother. She made her promise never to part with it. "You'll give it to your

own daughter one day!" she'd concluded. Ghizlane
turned as red as a tomato.

Mi-Lalla belonged to what passed for aristocracy
in Douar Scouila. The widow of a soldier who'd been
killed in Indochina, she received a monthly pension,
which, converted into dirhams, amounted to a tidy
sum. And since she hadn't stopped working and didn't
spend much, she'd managed to build up a decent nest
egg. No one knew where she had stashed her money;
her house, which was built of concrete, had been visited many times by burglars. One day she found her
garden completely dug up, since the thieves believed
she had buried her savings there. It was a waste of ef-
fort. Mi-Lalla's fortune lay in a safe place known only
to herself and God. Fuad used to say he'd rather not
find out, or it would be too tempting. That made Ghizlane laugh. She'd reply that he had many faults, but
stealing wasn't one of them. And anyway, she was going to ask Grandma's permission to start making cakes,
as she used to do, and he could sell them at the souk.
That way, he wouldn't have to ask anyone for money.
Now that he'd given up sniffing glue and had gone
back to soccer, he didn't have as many needs.

Mi-Lalla's work, as unpopular here as anywhere else,
made her a lot of enemies. She was a representative of
the law. Since men weren't allowed to enter people's
homes to make spot inventories of goods before they

were confiscated, it fell to mature women to do the job. It was a painful duty and the grandmother performed it reluctantly. She felt for these people who were about to have everything taken away because they were unable to pay their debts. Even after thirty years in the job, she still had scruples. Sometimes she'd send a messenger to warn her victims she'd be coming the next day. That way, they had time to move their most precious things during the night: their radio, television set, wool-filled mattresses . . . Even so, people avoided her like the plague. She was never invited to anyone's home, for fear she'd suddenly ask them to account for their furniture. People were too unkind, because Mi-Lalla had a big heart. It was true that she made her living from other people's misfortune, but it was a job, like any other. Gravediggers do the same, but they're still decent, honest people. I should know. As for me, I loved her as if she were a member of my family. She'd adopted me too, since I often came to play with her grandchildren. I called her Grandma like they did. She could see I was crazy about Ghizlane and it amused her. Coming across us sitting in a corner, she whispered: "One day, I'll marry the two of you." But before that, we had to behave ourselves. "Don't get up to any mischief, I'm watching you!" she called out, laughing.

Some temporary arrangements endure. The few weeks that Ghizlane and Fuad were meant to stay with Mi-Lalla turned into months, then into years. Halima came to see them less and less and they were none the worse for it. Her children avoided her. They'd be out when they knew she was coming. Soon the visits were limited to holidays and then they stopped for good. No one suffered too much, except perhaps Ghizlane, a little. She confided this to Mi-Lalla, who had a talent for soothing aching hearts with her magical phrase: "Tomorrow's light will open a different door." One tomorrow followed another and it turned out she was right: time eventually eased the little girl's distress.

Fuad now had a mobile stall measuring nearly one square meter, mounted on wheels that a blacksmith friend had made with great skill. He sold sweets, chocolates from Spain, lollipops, and Ghizlane's cakes. He'd set himself up at the entrance to the only school in the vicinity, and business was good.

Ghizlane had learned how to embroider and was working for the nuns, who provided her with fabric and good-quality thread. She'd make tablecloths, napkins, sheets, pillowcases, handkerchiefs, and linen of all kinds. You'd sometimes see luxury cars parked near the house. Women in European clothes, smelling strongly of perfume, would come to place orders with her. Mi-Lalla would tell her she ought to give some thought to her own trousseau, too, and Ghizlane would pretend to be annoyed.

I'd see her on Tuesdays, which was market day, and we'd go out together, wandering round the tent stalls that had been put up overnight. Douar Scouila's customary chaos would be multiplied a hundredfold. Men would jostle with beasts in happy confusion. And they'd be shouting, squabbling, laughing, guzzling, and belching all round the great mounds of brightly colored spices displayed on the ground, part of a vast throng: street vendors crying their wares, vying to make themselves heard above the din, chickens with their legs tied together cackling round farmers, braying donkeys collapsing under overloaded carts, a chanting chorus of blind men warning of Judgment Day. I knew every one of the thieves who operated round there. They weaved through the crowd, sharp-eyed and quick with their hands. We'd observe their maneuvering with glee: a deft slit of the razor on a back trouser pocket and they'd shadow their victim, patiently waiting for the wallet to drop. Ghizlane would laugh and give me a little tap on the back. Midday already. The aroma of grilled sausages, snail soup, and puréed broad beans was making us hungry. We'd buy ourselves a sandwich and devour it under a tree. Refreshed, we'd plunge back into the fray. Stopping by the fortune-tellers was obligatory, because Ghizlane was eager to find out everything there was to know. Those lowlifes were like weeds sprouting all over our misery. According to them, poverty would soon be abolished and love would reign supreme in Douar Scouila. They all but promised the resurrection of the dead. Ghizlane lapped up the good things foretold by the cards. Her eyes would light up the way they did in front of a fabric stall, when she'd start fingering and rummaging through the brightly colored materials, giving me a great many knowledgeable explanations about the provenance of the different wools, cottons, cloths, and satins. She'd criticize the prices and wouldn't buy much in the end. Or she'd spend hours haggling over a reel of thread. I'd be laughing and embarrassed at the same time. Sometimes she made me go to the barber—he too operated from a tent—because she thought I needed a haircut. Sitting on a stool, she waited, smiling at me in the mirror. She said that short hair really suited me; she thought I looked handsome. I thought she was beautiful too, but I didn't have the guts to say so. I once managed to stammer a compliment about her long black hair. She smiled. Walking side by side, our hands would brush and we'd pretend not to notice; we acted as if the shivers we felt were just chance, or the coolness of the morning. We'd stop at the stall selling sunflower seeds and buy ourselves a cone. She'd slip a note into my pocket, since she knew I was broke and thought it more proper for the man to pay. And she'd refuse to take it back. So we'd go on, wandering aimlessly, lingering in a crowd that had formed round a singer performing with his tam-tam. If she could have, she'd have danced with him. And the day would pass, as if in a dream. We'd be on our way home before sunset. Ghizlane didn't like to leave Mi-Lalla on her own too long; she was getting old and had more and more trouble keeping herself occupied. We'd bring her nougat, which she adored, though she could only suck it, since the stumps still clinging to her gums were about to fall out. If she'd had a good week, Ghizlane would bring her a scarf, a turban, or a prayer mat showing a sparkling Mecca. Mi-Lalla would instantly sniff back her tears. With age, she'd become very emotional.

That last evening, before the big day, we'd come back from the souk without saying much. Ghizlane hadn't laughed the whole walk home, which had gone quickly for me. She must have noticed the anguish my eyes couldn't hide. I'd have liked to walk and walk. I'd have liked to feel her slender fingers touch mine one last time, but we were already home. Right outside her house in the dark shadow of the blind alley, I took my courage in both hands and kissed her.

10

WHEN THE LIVING think about me, they open up a small window into their world. And I slip through on the quiet, not making a sound. I take care not to frighten them, otherwise they'll balk, throw up the dread walls of oblivion, and leave me confined in my purgatory, where I'm dying of boredom. That's why, as much as possible, I resist the temptation to intervene in earthly affairs. You're surprised, aren't you, that a wandering soul can interfere in the world of the living? Well, you'll just have to take my word for it. I'm not allowed to reveal any more than that. What I can say is that we possess a limited number of signs that we place along the paths of our nearest and dearest. So, as long as they bother to reflect on them, we have at least some scope for influencing particular situations. This can come about in different ways. Messages in dreams are the easiest for them to read, but on occasion, I admit, they can be quite disconcerting.

Sometimes I'm overcome by the urge to scream when I find misguided dreamers following in my footsteps; I have to force myself to abide by our rules. I want to tell them: all the promises they make you, however enticing, simply lead to death. So I suffer, in silence, and try to keep my demons in check. I sometimes tell myself that perhaps being unable to intervene fully and change things is itself hell, because I've been on fire since the day I died. Abu Zoubeir lied when he said we'd go straight to paradise. He used to say we'd already suffered our share of Gehenna in Sidi Moumen and therefore nothing worse could happen to us. And even that the faith he was instilling in us day after day was forging the shield that would enable us to step clear over the seven heavens to reach the light. He'd describe each stage, with its pitfalls, its temptations, its doubts and delirium. To hear him tell it, you could have sworn he'd died and come back to life ten times over, so intimately did he know every detail of the great journey, so deep was the conviction in his eyes as he related it.

In another garage, in another slum, there's the photo of me that Abu Zoubeir pinned to the wall alongside photos of the other martyrs: Nabil smiling beatifically; Khalil with a fixed grin; Blackie, his dark complexion

gone, staring with his wide protruding eyes and making a victory sign; and my brother Hamid, true to form,
displaying all the swagger of a born leader. This way,
Abu Zoubeir glorifies us forever in the fight against
the infidels. Looking at our portraits, other boys will
dream of justice and sacrifice, as we once did, watching
videos of the Palestinian or Chechen martyrs.

Abu Zoubeir, our spiritual guide, wasn't always
religious. For a long time he'd led a debauched life,
which he didn't attempt to hide. On the contrary, he'd
use it to convince us of the virtues of abstinence. He
could be completely objective because he'd been down
that road. Like many of the chosen ones who'd been
touched by grace, he'd fought a relentless battle against
the mediocrity of vice. Being close to the light, he was
now filled with inexpressible bliss, an inner peace superior in every way to that produced by hashish. Abu
Zoubeir knew the right words, the greedy words to
implant in the memory, which, as they grow, ingest all
the waste piled up there. He'd been born and raised in
Douar Lahjar, a shantytown even more run-down than
ours, if it's possible to compare derelictions. His en-
counter with God took place in Kenitra prison, where
he spent the best part of a decade. He didn't like to
talk about his crime, but we knew that rape and fraud
were involved. It was a period of his life he described
as supremely wayward. He used to say that prison had

saved him from himself; having the luck to meet men of faith there was a gift from heaven. So he felt obliged to give back some of the blessings he'd received. His new purpose was to help us purify our souls, to lead us on to the path of righteousness. In fact, that path led straight to death, our own and that of our fellow man, whom we were meant to love. Slam into a blind wall, surrounded by nothingness, where there's only regret, remorse, solitude, and desolation. Slam, slam, slam . . .

It felt good, being in the garage. The prayer mats on the walls were embroidered with verses from the Koran, in gold-thread calligraphy. The sparse furniture consisted of a raffia mat, a low table, a television, and a bookcase. Sitting cross-legged, dressed all in white, his beard carefully trimmed, Abu Zoubeir radiated a strange light. When his eyes rested on one of us, we had the impression he was reading our hearts, like a book. He had a sixth sense for discerning our innermost thoughts, our doubts, and our questions, to which he had clear and precise answers.

How old were we when those meetings began? Fifteen, maybe sixteen. Hamid was the first to start visiting Abu Zoubeir. I'd see them nattering away for hours over by the cesspools, near where we'd buried Morad. Hamid seemed fascinated by the eloquent conversation of his friend, whom he referred to as a guardian angel. To me he was more like a demon. In the beginning, I hated him, because my brother didn't notice me anymore, he ignored me. It was as if, overnight, I'd ceased to exist. Hamid was no longer interested in the Sunday games, or the fights that came after. Or even in his own business, which wasn't doing well. The boys he employed at the dump were stealing from him with complete impunity; but he couldn't care less. He'd lost all authority over the glue sniffers and his other flunkies, who'd gone freelance. Worse, he'd stopped getting high and, to crown it all, he'd begun to pray five times a day. The transformation was complete. Yemma was happy because he'd taken a job selling shoes in the city with a friend of Abu Zoubeir's. Nothing was the same as before. He'd bore the pants off us with his piety. On Fridays, he'd go to the mosque and take his place in the front row next to Abu Zoubeir, who'd then give a speech. He let his beard grow; he was the shadow of his former self. Gone was the dandy always up for a fight, sharp as a razor, organizing his own life and everyone else's. Mine especially. I'd grown up and could look after myself now, but I missed him. If, in a game, I made a spectacular save, I'd glance around for him, in case he was admiring my exploits from afar. I needed his applause, his yelling, his sudden storming of the field to give me a hug. But he wasn't there. His time was divided between the shop, the garage, and home, where he only came to eat. Gone, too, was the gaiety he usually spread around the table, the ridiculous stories that had Yemma in stitches. He could even extract a smile from my father's mummified face. He'd jeer at my brothers and no one would be able to get a word in edgeways, he was always so talkative, so funny. All that was gone. He managed to spin a kind of austere web that gradually entangled us all. We couldn't watch TV in peace because he'd be doing our heads in with his diatribes about the American-Zionist conspiracy that was brainwashing us all, corrupting our morals and insidiously infecting each one of us. Yemma didn't understand a word he was saying, but depriving her of her Egyptian and Brazilian soaps was out of the question. So, just to irritate us, he'd start noisily reciting the Koran in the room next door.

As time passed, Hamid would come home less and less. Eventually he set himself up in a shack near the garage, lent to him by Abu Zoubeir. That hurt a lot, because he left a gaping hole at home. I went on loving him in spite of it all. He was still my idol, on a par with Yachine, my soccer hero. I'd get up at dawn to go and meet him before he left for work. He'd take me to Belkabir's, a stallholder who made doughnuts that were second to none. Sitting behind a vast frying pan, the man with the spreading paunch would fling rounds of sticky dough into boiling oil. They'd instantly swell as they floated, giving off an exquisite smell. We'd buy a big crisp ring of them and take it to the café, order mint tea and happily munch away. Hamid said I ought to find myself a job so I'd be able to feed myself properly. He'd have a word with Abu Zoubeir, who had friends everywhere. I agreed, because I adored doughnuts. Sometimes he'd put me off my food by talking about hell so early in the morning. He'd insist that on the day of the Last Judgment the infidels would be thrown into vats of boiling oil, that their skin would keep growing back so they'd carry on frying and the suffering would be atrocious. That gave me goose bumps. I told him I believed in God and I'd never get fried like a doughnut. That's how I became an apprentice mechanic with Ba Moussa. A grubby job, but one I was conscientious about. And since Nabil was bored and kept hanging around the bikes I was fixing, he was taken on too. Together, we made a great team. So much so that Ba Moussa, who was an inveterate kif smoker, came to rely on us and we became *professionals*.

The shop consisted of two connecting rooms. The one at the back, which was tiny, dark, and airless, was where the boss lived. It had a bed and a table, on top of which, in pride of place, was a transistor radio, which blared from morning till night, and a suitcase for his clothes. A bare bulb, emitting a faint glow, hung from the low ceiling. We were always knocking our heads on it. The other room was our workshop: there was a crate full of tools, some old tires, nuts and bolts, screws, and a mountain of ill-assorted scrap metal that could be reused. But in fact, except when it rained, we always worked outside. The bicycle held no mysteries for us anymore. And then we progressed to the next stage: mopeds. That was a whole different story, but we knuckled down. Moussa would give us easy jobs to start with, and more complicated ones as we went on. And if, when we made a mistake, he took the liberty of giving us a beating, it was for our own good. We knew that. You have to be tough on apprentices at times, even if Ba Moussa, when he was annoyed, could deliver a real drubbing. I learned to keep out of the way, but Nabil had a knack for being in range. He bore the brunt of it. But hey, that was the deal.

It took us a few months to get the hang of the work. We learned to strip an engine in next to no time, lubricate it, replace the faulty parts, and reassemble it. I'd be ecstatic when an engine started up first time; I'd take it for a trial run on the tracks over at the dump. My friends, seeing me roar past, would howl with jealousy. Some of them threw stones and shouted: "Bourgeois filth!" I'd give them the finger and keep going. The boss was proud of us. As was Hamid, who'd come to visit, bringing bread, a tin of sardines, and potatoes. It was great. In those days, I was stuffing myself, spending half my salary on food. The rest I'd give to Yemma, who'd give it back to me in different ways. She bought balls of wool and knitted us jumpers, gloves, hats, and socks; she'd buy me a pair of espadrilles or anything else she could find at the souk that was cheap and useful. I'd put on weight and had grown about ten centimeters. It was all going so well. But in Sidi Moumen, the moment an engine is running smoothly, a bit of grit will get in to jam it. Without fail. It was woven into the fabric of our destinies.

If Nabil was a graceful creature, it wasn't his fault. If men did a double take as he walked by, he hadn't chosen to have a pert ass, or white skin, or silky curls. The older he got, the more desirable he became. I'm not saying I was immune to his charm. His feline, delicate beauty attracted me just as much as the others. I'm not saying I'd never considered it, but I'd quickly banish those appalling thoughts from my mind. The memory of that night in his shack with the Stars still makes my stomach heave. Nabil was dogged by bad luck, which is contagious. It was an easy life, for sure, now that we were no longer scavenging on the dump. We had a cushy job that brought in a hundred dirhams a week and elevated us to the rank of princes. Not for a moment did giving it up cross our minds. But that damned ass of Nabil's only ever caused us grief.

One evening, when he was staying late at the shop to fix a bike, Ba Moussa came back from prayers and lowered the metal grille. He took off his djellaba and went over to Nabil, who instantly recognized the look in his boss's eyes. He stayed on his guard, going on with his work as if nothing were amiss. Ba Moussa's voice was soft and syrupy, quite different from his daytime one, which was harsh and grating. He leaned over him and pinched his cheeks: "You know you're a beautiful boy!" Without thinking for a second, Nabil grabbed the wrench in his grease-blackened hands and struck him violently on the temple. A muffled, frightening sound, and the man's full weight fell on the scrap metal. No doubt it was panic that had unleashed Nabil's strength, to make him knock him out like that. He might have left it there, pulled up the grille and walked out. Events might have taken a different turn. A reconciliation might have been possible the next day: a couple of slaps and order would have been restored. But Nabil was in the grip of some demon that made him go on with the attack and lay into his aggressor, who was lying on the ground, barely conscious. He bent over him and, blinded with rage, pounded him again and again, shattering his skull. And as if that weren't enough, he seized a hammer that was lying around and began to batter him furiously in the balls. He was battering the man but also the fate that had condemned him from birth. The spurting blood only excited him more. And he went on until he was exhausted, until he could no longer hold the tool in his hand; then he lay down on top of the boss and stayed there motionless a long while, like a wild beast, sated, slumped over its prey.

Seeing him a few hours later, not far from where we lived, I was afraid. His face was pale, his clothes were soaked in blood, and he was incapable of uttering a word. I brought him a glass of water and we sat down on the step by our door. It took a long time for him to pull himself together, then, with unnerving calm, he said:

"I've killed the boss."

I was stunned.

"Are you sure?"

"I hit him hard, very hard, the disgusting pig."

"Maybe you just knocked him out."

Nabil looked down and didn't answer. I realized that he was serious and that that meant the end of our stint as mechanics. Together we went to explain the situation to my brother Hamid, who, once again calling on his garage friends, rescued us from that nightmare. Ba Moussa was buried in the dump that same night, near where Morad lay. And to avoid the risk of anyone finding the two corpses, they set fire to the whole area. We'd gone with them and it was a beautiful sight, the fire in the night. It crackled, it glowed red. The high flames pierced the black sky and, as we danced under the gaze of the silent stars, our deformed shadows trailed over the filth. Abu Zoubeir and Hamid said a prayer. I'd have liked to join in, but I didn't know the words. I was afraid the fire would spread and said so to Hamid, who dismissed the idea with a wave of his hand, since it had rained the day before. I wasn't entirely reassured. Thinking about it, he was right. He knew the dump better than anyone. Little by little, the flames died out, as if they were tired, over the ashes of Morad and the boss. On the way back, we barely spoke. Near Omar the coalman's shop, Abu Zoubeir turned to my brother and said: "You ought to invite them to the garage! It would do them good to be closer to God." Hamid agreed.

Apart from a distant cousin who visited him once a year, Ba Moussa didn't have any family. So no one asked questions about his disappearance. Besides, the denizens of Sidi Moumen were used to people moving in and out in a hurry. People come and go without anyone really knowing why. Others take their place, make a home in an empty hovel, improvise, adapt, and maintain the general decrepitude, as if to ensure the survival of our species.

After he'd cleaned the shop, Hamid brought us the crate of tools, saying that it might be useful, seeing as we'd learned the trade. He advised us to clear off, make ourselves scarce until things settled down. Which we did. And life resumed its course, as if old Moussa had never existed.

11

GHIZLANE DID NOT appreciate my going to live with Nabil. I reckon she was jealous; she'd have liked to take his place. Yemma, too, was hurt by my decision to leave. She cried the day I broke the news. My brothers had left, one after the other, heading for the city or joining the army; three of them had gotten married and built their own homes in Chichane. There was only Said left to support her. Said was a lovely boy. A bit simple, it's true, but he didn't bother anyone. You barely noticed he was there; he was almost transparent. Never the least complaint out of him. To him, Yemma's cooking was delicious even when she put far too much spice in it. We could gauge my mother's mood by the amount of salt she used. An oversalted tagine meant we'd better watch out: it had been a bad day and the slightest misdemeanor would lead to a beating. Said did all the hardest jobs

without ever making a fuss. Yemma wasn't fair to him,
she was always shouting at him because he got everything wrong. Sometimes she'd feel bad about it and, by
way of an apology, she'd slip a few dirhams in his pocket.
"Clear off! Go outside for a bit! I can't have you under
my feet all day." Said would walk all round the shacks
and come back a quarter of an hour later, sitting down
next to my father to play checkers. The streets fright-
ened him; he felt better at home with his transistor radio
and his faded newspapers. He never tired of the mining
stories my father endlessly regurgitated, which had different versions depending on how ill he felt. Said would
follow the news with unswerving attention, as if the future of the planet depended on him. He commented
on events, supplying his precious analysis, without realizing that Father was practically deaf and Yemma didn't
understand a thing about politics. But at least he'd talk
about issues beyond the usual concerns: "The roof's
leaking," "The water from the pump smells bad," "The
price of oil, sugar, or tea has gone up," "The pirate sta-
tions have been scrambled . . ." Anyway, I was glad he'd
stayed at home. I was sixteen and my shoulders were
broader than Hamid's. It was time I started fending for
myself like other boys my age.

Nabil and I had decorated the shack as best we
could, the way we'd dreamed about in the old days. My
brother and Abu Zoubeir had given us a substantial

sum of money to set ourselves up; a generous dona-
tion, which was deeply touching. It meant we could
buy a straw mattress, a pillow, a woolen blanket, and
a strong zinc sheet to reinforce the roof. We allowed
ourselves one treat: a radio-cassette player, almost new,
because the old one was well and truly dead. So we organized ourselves and shared the workload. Nabil was
in charge of the cooking and I'd work as a mechanic.
I'd picked up an old wheel from a cart and wedged
it between two big stones on the street to show that
repairs were done there. Since everyone knew us, we
took over Ba Moussa's trade. If Nabil had finished his
chores early and the tagine was simmering on the brazier, he'd come and give me a hand. He'd mostly patch
up flat tires. And business was pretty good, thanks to
the shards of broken bottles, scraps of metal, and sharp
stones that littered the paths. I'd built up an impressive
stock of equipment. We'd dismantle mopeds that had
been stolen in the city and sell off the separate parts
at prices that were absolutely unbeatable, so a large
portion of our profits would be reinvested. I was a past
master in the art of recycling and DIY. Whatever the
problem, we had the solution. And we had a lot on our
plate because Sidi Moumen's two-wheelers were in a
hopeless state of disrepair. However old, however broken down, even falling to pieces, we'd find them happy
owners who'd torture them for a few more years. They

made me think of the buses the French would sell on to us after a lifetime of good and loyal service in the motherland, which we'd use for at least a decade before palming them off on the Africans, who could eke out of them a few more fine days in the bush.

We played soccer less and less, but our shack was still the Stars of Sidi Moumen's HQ. Friends would come by in the evenings to hang out with us. We'd started drinking red wine. It was cheap plonk but it suited us. If we'd done well that day, we'd have a round of beers, which we'd buy by the case. Khalil the shoeshine had done time for stealing from a foreigner. He claimed he was innocent, saying he'd found the wallet on the ground after he'd polished the tourist's shoes. The police didn't see it that way and he got three months behind bars. Khalil was seething with rage. He wanted to leave, go to Europe, where people had rights. And if, by some mishap, someone was wrongly accused, they'd get a fortune in compensation. Yes, he was very seriously thinking of getting together the necessary amount to slip across to Spain and leave this godforsaken country. But there was that story his cousin had told us about what happened to illegal immigrants, which wasn't exactly encouraging. On a northern beach, as he waited for the crossing to Algeciras, he'd come across the corpse of a sub-Saharan hopeful, spewed up by the tide. A colossus of a man, whose facial features had almost completely disappeared. He'd lost a shoe and the fish had nibbled away his toes. A small crab was clambering out of his left eye. Khalil's cousin had seen this and had given up the idea of leaving. He'd said: "You see, even the crabs wanted nothing to do with that African!"

Khalil didn't like that story; he said that you could die anywhere—on a sidewalk, by falling out of bed, or swallowing something the wrong way. In any case, he was sticking to his plan. He said the police were scum because they'd beaten him up to make him admit to his crime. He'd finally signed his confession, but it wasn't true at all. He'd have confessed to anything to make them stop punching him. They'd threatened to make him sit on a Coca-Cola bottle if he didn't spill the beans. They'd taken him down to a dark cellar and shown him the pliers they'd use to pull out his nails and the electric wires they'd connect to his balls. But a couple of hard slaps and a kick had done the job. So he'd signed and signed again because the tourist in question happened to be the French consul. In court, it had all been over in five minutes, and the judges were scum too. Just like the screws, who'd roughed him up all through his interminable stay in prison.

Khalil was raging at the entire world and after one too many he was a different animal. Between us we'd tear limb from limb the judges, the police, the screws,

and all the consuls on the planet. We let him talk because it made him feel better. When his face relaxed,
we'd follow him in his reveries, over the Strait of Gi-
braltar on a makeshift raft, and Spain would be ours
for the taking. Oh, those gorgeous Andalusian wom-
en, our long-lost cousins, all forlorn and yearning to
be our future conquests. But Paris, only Paris really
counted. Khalil would serve us up the "Champs-Ely-
sées," "Saint-Germain-des-Prés," "Sacré-Coeur," and
the "Eiffel Tower": garlanded names he'd picked up
here and there, which we'd repeat all together, the way
we'd learned our lessons in the Koranic school when
we were small. We'd clap our hands when fortune
smiled on us—when Khalil described the scene of his
return to Sidi Moumen, in a brand-new station wagon
with a blonde at his side and an electric guitar on the
backseat. The idea of marrying a European woman,
suitably fattened up on hormones, made him hard.
He'd take out his stiff, fat cock and bang it on the table,
saying: "And this, this is my passport to paradise!" And
we'd fall about like kids. Khalil wanted to be an artist
too. He'd gotten that from an American soap opera he
must have watched on TV; he'd slipped inside the hero's
skin and refused to get out. When the drink went to
his head, he'd start singing in a strange new language,
with an English accent, prancing around and playing
air guitar. Nabil couldn't help jigging up and down

with him and said we ought to form a band; we'd be so famous the whole wide world would be open to us. Talent breaks down borders, everyone knows that, so we wouldn't need visas, or any other proof, to enter the Garden of Eden . . .

Dreams, too, are contagious.

Ghizlane would come to cook for us on Fridays. She'd bring a basket of vegetables and some mutton. Nabil would help her and the two of them would prepare meals fit for a king. Her specialty was barley couscous. We'd sit round a huge earthenware dish and have a feast. Fuad would join us after school with his mobile stall, which he'd park indoors. He'd pretend to be furious when we nicked sweets from him. He'd chase us down the street and Ghizlane would laugh like a little girl. Sometimes she'd surprise us, whisking from her basket cakes that would melt in the mouth. We'd savor them outside in the sunshine. Ghizlane was growing more and more beautiful. I'd look at her breasts, which her loose smocks weren't able to hide. They were two pears, almost ripe, with raisins on top, which poked at the embroidered cloth and seemed frustrated that they couldn't come out into the open. I could tell they were unhappy, those pears, and dreamed of consoling them with a thousand caresses, of biting into their soft flesh, burying my nose and my senses in them and losing myself there. Ghizlane noticed my insistent stares and pretended she hadn't. I could tell by the pupils of her eyes, which were slightly dilated, and the way she smoothed down her hair.

It was a wondrous time, I realize now, when everything seemed to come together as if by magic.

Blackie had at last rebelled and left his father's shop. One day when Omar the coalman, over some nonsense, had raised his hand to slap him, Blackie had grabbed it and squeezed hard, signaling that he'd no longer allow himself to be beaten, and then let go, looking his father straight in the eye. It was a breathtaking moment, without precedent in the two men's lives. Omar the coalman was suddenly aware that he was losing a second child. Blackie had grown up, he was white again because he'd gradually deserted the shop. He was a good head taller than his father. He too had understood that the estrangement was complete. It wasn't premeditated, but it had happened. Helpless and weary, sitting on a stool between sacks of coal, Omar silently watched his son leave.

When Blackie showed up at our place with his belongings, we of course welcomed him. It was a summer evening and I remember we were sitting on the doorstep smoking kif. The moon was round and so white that we could not make out the features of our late king, who was supposed to be visible in it. Blackie sat down opposite me and I saw the light bathe his sad face. He smoked with us and started to feel better. We chatted idly, with no mention of his father. I'd been afraid of this moment, but I had no choice: leaving my friend on the street was out of the question. Nabil invited him in, pointed to a sheepskin, a blanket, and a cushion and said: "Take them, they're yours." And now there were three of us in the shack. It was cramped, but no one complained. Blackie tried to make himself as unobtrusive as possible, so he wouldn't be any trouble. He helped Nabil with the cleaning and did the shopping in Douar Scouila on market days. The rest of the time, he'd do odd jobs here and there to make a bit of money and contribute to household expenses. Nabil and Blackie slept in one room and I slept in the other. My brother's behavior had rubbed off on me, because I became, in a way, the head of the family. That authority over my friends had come about without my having to impose it. My decisions were followed to the letter because they made sense (or so I thought at the time). And that's why, when Hamid persuaded me to attend the classes that Abu Zoubeir was giving at the garage, they all came with me, unquestioningly. So began our slippery descent into a world that was not our own. A new world that would suck us in deeper and deeper and finally swallow us for good.

12

THERE WERE FOUR of them, the emir and his companions. They had odd names, all beginning with "Abu" something. Exotic names, reminiscent of the days of the Prophet. To be brief, I'll call them by the "something": Zaid, Nouceir, and the Oubaida brothers, Ahmed and Reda.

The oldest, and probably the most erudite, was Emir Zaid, who was twenty-five but seemed older because of the thick beard that covered three-quarters of his face. He always wore a big pair of horn-rimmed glasses, a crocheted skullcap, and a white robe, so he looked almost interchangeable with any one of his comrades. Originally from the north of the country, for some unknown reason he'd wound up in the Chichane slum. Nothing was known about his family or how he'd come to undertake his studies. But in any case, he was knowledgeable in many areas of scholarship. We could ask him anything and he'd be able to answer, or if he wasn't sure, he'd bring us precise information the following day. He had a serious, soft voice, a welcoming expression, and he always rested his hand on the shoulder of whomever he was with, as a sign of brotherhood. Seeing him in the street, no one would suspect that this chubby-faced man of average height was in fact a master of martial arts. He had done his training outside Morocco. Some said in China, others Japan, but in any case, light years from Sidi Moumen. Abu Zoubeir showed him a certain deference, as did my brother Hamid. Zaid was particularly interested in young people, meaning my friends and me. He nobly offered to teach us kung fu techniques. Nabil was over the moon. He'd always dreamed of being able to defend himself, and the emir was offering him this priceless gift on a plate. He'd wake me early in the morning and drag me off to a place near the garage where I'd do my exercises and say my first prayers, too—a prerequisite for participating in training sessions.

Khalil the shoeshine and Blackie joined us and soon we were all caught up in it. We'd meet in a windowless room, in a concrete building. The floor and some of the walls were covered in raffia mats, with a silk carpet at the back, where Zaid would sit, holding a string of beads that he'd wind round his wrist during the class. It was like a miniature mosque. It had the kind of silence that befitted a place of worship, where you feel the Lord's presence more keenly than anywhere else. The samurai bow was accompanied by a verse from the Koran, so we'd begin our warm-ups in quasi-religious fervor. Then came the collective kata, where we'd fight invisible adversaries in the name of Allah. We had to wait several weeks before starting to fight properly. But even then, we didn't hit anyone in the face; we held back before impact, which was a massive change from our usual fist-fights. We learned self-control, the art of evasion, and discipline. But at the end of the class, as soon as Zaid left the room, we'd hurl ourselves on top of each other in riotous scrums. We had great fun imitating Bruce Lee in *Fist of Fury*, and made ourselves copies of his lethal weapon: two bits of wood linked by a chain. Nouceir taught us the countless ways to handle them. It wasn't easy at first. We'd get hit all over our faces and bodies. Which made us laugh, despite the pain. Not to blow my own trumpet, but after a few weeks I was a wizard with that thing. Our whole time was spent leaping in the air, executing spectacular combat positions, but we were a long way from Bruce Lee's acrobatics. Nouceir used to say that the master's flying leaps were cinematographic effects, but we weren't convinced. When his films were shown on TV, we'd ensconce ourselves in the café and watch them religiously, as if they were soccer games. Like our hero, we too wanted to right wrongs, avenge the weak, and restore justice. Zaid agreed with us, but repeated that there were different ways to change the world. The main thing was to use our brains. He claimed that it was never too late to learn, to perfect ourselves, and drive out the darkness that threatened us. The advantage of kung fu, he added, consists in turning the stronger man's weapon against him. That was why Bruce Lee, who was smaller and less muscular than his enemies, always overcame them in the end. He said that Allah was just, that He loved justice. But I wasn't so sure. If that were so, how do you account for places like Sidi Moumen? Zaid said the fault lay with men, who'd turned away from the divine message. Whatever the truth, we were so enthusiastic that we never once missed a training session.

These sessions were starting earlier and earlier. We'd make sure to do our ablutions and say our prayers together, at dawn, after the muezzin's call. If Yemma could have seen us, she wouldn't have believed her eyes. Hamid and I, at first light, standing in the middle of a room packed with the faithful at prayer. She'd have been proud to see us putting on our brand-new kimonos, which were presents from Abu Zoubeir. Hamid would choose me as his adversary in combat, which I loved. Fuad had joined us in the end, because he wanted to learn to fight too. And since he lived in Douar

Scouila, he'd often sleep over at our place. I'd let him have a corner of my room and he was happy there. Now there were four of us in a tight space; it reminded me of the hovel I'd grown up in. Still, we were always outside. Between sport, bike repairs, our evenings at the garage, and praying five times a day, we didn't have time to catch our breath. We'd stopped drinking alcohol because we didn't dare anymore. Maybe a joint from time to time, but we kept it quiet. In any case, we were so tired in the evenings that we only wanted to sleep. And I can tell you, we might have been in a flophouse, our snoring was so loud.

Nouceir was Zaid's cousin. In fact, they weren't really cousins, they just came from the same village, up near Larache. He was the only one of the emir's companions with whom I had anything in common. Not much older than me, he'd been goalie for the Chichane team. We both hero-worshipped Yachine; we could talk about him for hours. We'd had to be rivals in the old days, but that was all in the past. He had a soft spot for Ghizlane too, but backed off as soon as he found out she was meant for me. He avoided looking at her directly when we met on Fridays after prayers. Now there was a crowd of us eating couscous outside the shack. Beggars would be hanging around and we'd invite them to join us whenever we could. To get some peace, we decided to make a separate bowl for them. Otherwise it would be a free-for-all; their big paws would grope around in the couscous to get to the meat. They seemed hungrier than us and they ate very fast.

Fuad had moved in permanently, which was the perfect pretext for Ghizlane, who'd come to visit twice a week and more on holidays. She'd made us green velvet curtains, and sheets, which we didn't dare use, since we'd never had any before. The place had a woman's touch: now there were plastic flowers in a superb gilt vase and photo frames for our pictures. Nouceir had brought over a wool carpet, which was a present from Zaid. It was more comfortable for group prayers. Our shack became a cheerful, convivial place. If Hamid gave us a bit of incense, it smelled like paradise. We listened to cassettes of the Koran and speeches by oriental sages. They comforted us. The emir and his companions were simple people, who sometimes did us the honor of coming to visit, filling us with light and peace. Hamid was proud of me; I could see it in his eyes. Sometimes Abu Zoubeir himself would join us. And it was like a victory over our mediocre, small lives. We'd drink in everything he said, because we understood him. He'd given us back our pride with simple words, winged words that carried us as far as our imaginations could go. No longer were we parasites, the dregs of humanity, less than nothing. We were clean and deserving and our aspirations resonated with healthy minds. We were listened to, guided.

Logic had taken the place of beatings. We had opened
the door to God and He had entered into us. No more
chasing around frantically, expending pointless energy,
no more insults and stupid brawling. No more living
like cockroaches on the excrement of heretics. Gone, the
fatalism injected in our veins by our uneducated parents.
We learned to stand shoulder to shoulder, to flatly refuse
the worm's life to which we'd been condemned in per-
petuity. We knew that rights weren't given, they had to
be seized. And we were ready for any sacrifice. Friday
became a real day for celebration in Sidi Moumen.

Ghizlane wasn't so happy, because she'd suddenly
been excluded from our circle. She'd still come to make
couscous for us and then go back to Mi-Lalla's. That
hurt, but I didn't show it. Sometimes I'd go to see her
in Douar Scouila. She said I'd changed, and reproached
me for neglecting my parents, which was very bad, since
my mother was unhappy. I had trouble explaining to her
how I felt. I simply replied that God was great and He'd
make everything all right in the end. She said that God
had nothing to do with it, that parents were sacred, even
bad ones. Mi-Lalla claimed that paradise lay beneath
mothers' feet, that to get there, you had to kneel down
and kiss the soles of those feet every morning. Ghizlane
told me my beard made my face look hard and it didn't
suit me at all. I promised her I'd shave it off. It wasn't
compulsory anyway; I'd only grown it to look like Zaid.

We all tried to copy the emir. She complained about her brother, who was hassling her to cover her hair. I didn't agree with him, even though it wouldn't detract from her beauty. I said I'd have a word with him, that there was no point falling out over something so small. Her beautiful hair definitely didn't deserve to be imprisoned by a bit of cloth and I didn't see what was so provocative about it. I asked Zaid about it one evening in the garage, after prayers. He replied that a woman who sought to tempt men did not deserve respect, because temptation is Satan's province. That this was an ancestral value that evil minds sought to deny. He added that, in order to preserve our identity, we must follow the path trodden by the Prophet Muhammad, peace and salvation be upon Him. That dissuaded me from taking it any further. I felt that a woman's eyes were far more alluring than her hair, anyway; but if I'd said so, he'd have advocated the burka. At least with a veil you could cheat a bit, depending how you wore it. And, on the whole, some of the colored scarves weren't so bad. So in the end I asked Fuad to leave his sister alone; it was simpler.

Weeks and months went by with us living on top of each other in this way. Everything was regulated, measured, weighed. I more or less gave up the bike repairs, since our evenings at the garage went on later and later. We learned the Koran by heart. It wasn't that hard. Abu Zoubeir would analyze its innumerable aspects. He'd launch into passionate explanations and commentaries. The life of the Prophet was now an open book. Our hearts quivered to the rhythm of his conquests, which God planned in advance. We knew that the battle the crusaders and the Jews were waging against us was insidious. And sometimes completely blatant. Jihad was our only salvation. God demanded it of us. It was written, in black and white, in the book of books.

13

THE OUBAIDA BROTHERS were unrivaled mechanics, capable of dismantling and rebuilding any device known to man. They'd repair just about anything they were presented with: radios, TVs, satellite dishes, hair dryers, watches, computers. And for free. Which is another way of saying there was always a line at the door of the Internet café they'd opened at the entrance to the slum. In Sidi Moumen, faulty appliances were legion. As well as stuff you might salvage at the dump, the gadgets from Asia, which were alluring but cheap, were constantly breaking. The two men never turned down a job. At Hamid's request, they hired Fuad, who was tired of his paltry sweet sales outside the school. He became a security guard at their café, a position created just for him, since there was no chance anyone round there would dream of stealing from them, they were so popular. Had elections not stopped at the slum walls (because people no longer believed in them), the Oubaida brothers would have won hands down and been elected presidents for life in Sidi Moumen, as they would in any self-respecting Arab country. At last, Fuad had a weekly salary and it changed his life. He bought himself a bicycle, which I fixed up to look brand-new, attaching a rearview mirror, a two-tone bell, and an old mudguard that had been lying around the shack. Ghizlane was overjoyed, she kissed my brother's hands every time she ran into him.

Khalil the shoeshine found a job too, with a friend of Emir Zaid's, at a printing press in the city. It was cushy work; he didn't have to deal with café waiters, loutish racketeers, or police batons. He was entitled to leave the workshop at prayer times and, best of all, he could eat with the staff. In his wildest dreams he could never have imagined that. Three hearty meals a day! And he was the greedy type. He not only ate his share, but pounced on the leftovers on his fellow workers' trays too. He'd mop their plates clean with bread rolls and drain all the glasses of Coca-Cola to the last drop. As for Nabil and me, we gave up bike repairs for good and became Abu Zoubeir's messengers. We were glad to serve the master; many of the others envied us our closeness to him. We did all the cleaning at the garage and Nabil made the tea.

All the families of garage regulars were given a basket of food every day, but Yemma still found grounds
to complain about how rarely we visited. One day I
brought her a sheep, as the holiday was approaching.
She burst into tears, not from joy at the sight of the
struggling ram with its big horns, but from emotion at
my presence. Seeing me all clean and handsome in my
white robe, my beard cut Afghan-style, she took me for
Hamid. She was angry with herself for this and sobbed
some more. And she cried more than ever when my
brother arrived halfway through the afternoon. Yemma
spoke less and less and cried over nothing. Old people
weep easily because they're more conscious of time passing. They become emotional over the smallest thing.

Now that I'm up here, unraveling my past like a ball
of wool, full of knots, I think she must have foreseen
the fatal outcome of our adventure. Yet she had no
idea of the mess we'd gotten ourselves into. Maybe it
was that sixth sense Mi-Lalla used to talk about. In
any case, that day she shut herself up in the kitchen to
make the tea and stayed there longer than usual. She
didn't want to cause us any pain. Hamid and I promised to come and slaughter the sheep ourselves and
she smiled. It was so good to see her smile. Said was
happy to see us, since he could bore us witless with his
rants on politics. Iraq, Afghanistan, Chechnya, Rwan-
da: you name it, he was onto it. With a sprinkling of

earthquakes, deadly epidemics, and tsunamis for good measure. I refused to meet Hamid's eye so as not to burst out laughing. Father was constantly sneezing, snorting his cheap snuff. He offered me some for the first time, a sign that he now saw me as an adult. I accepted, even though I didn't like it. And we sneezed together. Like brothers. Seeing my nose smeared with powder and my bloodshot eyes, Hamid erupted into booming laughter, like in the old days. It had been an age since I'd heard him laugh. So I laughed too. And then we all laughed. It was laughter from the belly and the heart, the laughter of people who'd been starved of laughter; the reason for it scarcely mattered, it felt unbelievably good. And it went on and intensified until it turned into nervous laughter. Yemma started crying again. In fact, we couldn't tell anymore if they were tears of joy or sadness; she was laughing and crying at the same time. And then we all were. We cried and laughed until we could cry and laugh no more. It was good laughter, family laughter. My father was squawking like a bird and I thought he was going to choke. Said was beaming and kept punching the cushion. He said we should all get together more often to have a laugh, even if the international situation wasn't favorable. And Hamid was off again, laughing his legendary laugh.

That was the last time I saw my parents.

It was a very busy period. One night, people I didn't know came to the garage to talk with the master. Abu Zoubeir, who normally dismissed us when he had important visitors, asked us to stay. Nabil, Hamid, and I felt flattered; we took it as a promotion in our secret struggle to be closer to the master. Now we were part of the inner circle. Abu Zoubeir consulted us on all kinds of subjects and seemed to take notice of our opinions. I'd keep my mouth shut, for fear of coming out with something stupid, but Nabil didn't hold back, launching into damning condemnations of American or Israeli attacks. Abu Zoubeir agreed with him, and I admit I was a bit jealous. Luckily, my brother Hamid was there to fly the flag for our family and went one better, blasting the crusaders and the Jews. Better yet, he attacked Arab regimes that had no dignity, prostrate as they were before their Western overlords, their sole aim to perpetuate their dictatorships. I nodded my agreement; Hamid was completely right.

The television was turned to a channel that showed massacres of Muslims on a loop. And that made our blood boil, I can tell you. The little Palestinian boy in his father's arms had died a hundred times. Every time he died, we had tears in our eyes. And rage sweated from all the pores of our rigid bodies as the loop showed the slaughter again and again. We saw soldiers, bristling with weapons, shooting blindly at people throwing stones, and we wanted to strangle them. The child was dead all right, but his father didn't relax his grip, as if he were still alive. As if the piercing screams he'd uttered a few minutes before were still ripping through the uproar of shooting and people in panic. Abu Zoubeir said we had to react. The Prophet would never have tolerated such humiliation. Sitting cross-legged before the master, I felt fire flare in my belly, setting my eyes ablaze. A thirst for vengeance twisted my guts. We were ready to redeem our lost honor in blood. We weren't losers or cowards. Still less door-mats, on which repulsive heathens and our country's corrupt wiped their feet.

Abu Zoubeir's friends observed us with an air of satisfaction. One of them, probably their leader, was an elderly man, impressively tall in his turban and a white djellaba. He smelled of sandalwood, like the perfume Hamid used to bring back for Yemma. He closed his eyes and made a speech. It was about hope, about Ji-had, about light. While there were still men like us, young, brave, with conviction, all was not lost. Satan's henchmen had it coming. They would pay a hundred times over for what they were making us suffer. We would make their lives hell. Their sophisticated arsenals would be obsolete and ridiculous. God was with us and victory was within our grasp. We had weapons the unbelievers did not: our flesh and our blood. We would return them to God; He demanded them of us. Our sacrifices would be rewarded. The gates to heaven were wide open and beckoning. Those blasphemers could only tremble in their foul pigsties, in their debauched, abject lives, determined as they were to infect our children with their impurity . . . Then he stopped talking. Stroking his beard, the sheikh cast his eyes over our faces, which were all lit up, and said: "You cannot defeat a man who wants to die!"

After a communal prayer, he stretched out his hand, which we all kissed in turn. And we never saw him at the garage again.

The sheikh's face would haunt us for a long time. I remember the strange scene on the doorstep before he left. Abu Zoubeir knelt down and kissed his slippers as if paradise lay beneath them. The sheikh helped him to his feet and embraced him. He whispered in his ear something we couldn't hear. But as he came back in, Abu Zoubeir's eyes were red, as if he'd been crying.

14

ONE EVENING, HAMID arrived at the shack to tell us the good news: Abu Zoubeir was treating us to a holiday. Now that was a word that didn't figure in our vocabulary. It sounded so sweet to our ears! Although, to go on holiday implied we'd been working hard and our bodies were crying out for rest, which hadn't been the case for some time now. Life in the garage was easy: we recited the Koran, we prayed, we listened, we ate properly, and we slept. We were outside the world, as if in a chrysalis, attuned to the master's wisdom and our own untroubled hearts. But the decision had been made and we were thrilled. Everything had been arranged and thought out down to the last detail: a small van would come to pick us up the next day to take us to the mountains, because Abu Zoubeir wanted to thank us for our diligence in his classes. Nabil started dancing in the middle of the room;

he couldn't express his joy any other way. Hamid said that we were all invited and that it would last a whole week. Khalil and Fuad were immediately given leave from the printing press and the Internet café without any deduction from their pay. "A present is a present!" Hamid added. Nabil, Blackie, and I had trouble sleeping that night, we were so excited by the idea of the trip. We'd packed our bags, remembering toiletries, kimonos, and our djellabas, in case it was cold up there. It was the first time I'd be leaving Sidi Moumen, or riding in a van. Seeing as he was no stranger to police vans, Khalil couldn't say the same.

The minibus turned up at seven in the morning, as arranged, outside the Oubaida brothers' café. We were on time; none of us was going to miss this. We boarded the bus and took our places behind Emir Zaid, who'd been concealing from us his skills as a driver. There were three rows of black leather seats. I sat up front to get the best view of the countryside. The journey would take all day. "The Middle Atlas isn't exactly round the corner," the emir had explained. We were soon out of Sidi Moumen. It was getting hot already but not in our *air-conditioned* vehicle; that meant you could go from summer to winter at the flick of a switch. We drove through Casablanca and the emir made a detour through the big boulevards to show us Anfa, the poshest neighborhood in the whole country.

It's hard to describe that part of the city, as we couldn't see much. We could barely make out the lavish houses through the walls of thick foliage, which was dotted with curious flowers, like purple, red, and yellow bells, and farther off, brightly colored sprays with complicated shapes; I had a weakness for those little white flowers with the surprising scent. I opened the window to inhale the smell. The emir, who knew everything, told me they were jasmine. I thought the name suited the flower and said: "I love jasmine." I wondered why these pretty plants didn't grow where we lived, since we had the soil and the water; a few cuttings would be enough to cheer up our lives. Quite a few people grew plants in front of their shacks, but they were never so beautiful, or so sweet-smelling. Maybe it wouldn't suit jasmine to be so close to the dump. A flower as delicate as that would commit suicide, the stink was so suffocating. It would be almost an insult to its sweet fragrance.

We seemed to be flying as we drove. We didn't feel any jolts, as there were no potholes in the freshly tar-macked streets. The roads were wide and clean. Cars straight out of the future were parked here and there. The emir cruised along slowly, letting us take in the beauty all around us. Then he headed for the coast road and we saw the sea. It was an extraordinary sight. This different air was making me dizzy; it had a funny smell. I shivered, staring at the infinite silvery blue, with the white sun floating above. Seagulls, craftier than the ones in Sidi Moumen, were trailing a boat that must be taking people to Spain. Khalil was gazing at the ship and I think in his mind he was on it. People told so many stories about stowaways who hid in the cargo hold to flee the country. But he'd have wanted to be standing on the deck, in full sunlight. The whole atmosphere radiated happiness. Yet we weren't so far from Sidi Moumen: a quarter of an hour by car, at most. Of course, our buses didn't go to the rich parts of town, so our kind of people wouldn't pollute this elegant environment. Which I completely under-stand, because we were incapable of keeping a place as clean as this. And the jasmine, like the bellflowers, would have been picked and sold by the bunch. Or just uprooted for the fun of it. All the houses would have been burgled, in spite of the security guards with their big sticks who watched over every one of them. And no doubt envious people would have gone and set fire to them. Emir Zaid said that we were in the stronghold of Satan's lackeys, that the infidels who shut themselves away here owned three-quarters of the country's wealth. And the fact that we lived in utter destitution was because of these leeches, who'd made pacts with the Western devils to exploit us and keep us in a state of total dependence. Without them, we die.

But without us, they too are doomed to certain death. Because they need a docile workforce, and blood to suck. They kill us by degrees. But if we have to die, we might as well take them with us and have done with it, once and for all . . .

We'd never seen the emir get so carried away. He realized this, and went on in a more subdued tone, but the light still gleamed in his eyes: "We must join forces and ask for God's help. They are already trembling at the sight of our beards—let us flaunt them! Let them hide away in their gilded cages with their vile offspring, their depraved wives and corrupt morals. They can slob about on their silk sofas with their fat pig bellies all they like, getting drunk on the sweat from our brows; the streets will be ours in the end. And they'll have to be accountable one way or another, down here or in heaven! We will not forgive them." Then together we recited a graphic verse detailing the horror that awaited unbelievers in hell.

After the satanic paradise of Anfa, we drove through the chaos of the city. My only memories are of frazzled people in a hurry, endlessly blaring their horns. Drivers argued and shook their fists. Those on foot crossed wherever they could, however they could, and were quick to complain, too, when no one gave way. Police officers blew their whistles left, right, and center and the motorists couldn't care less. The emir was calmer now and drove carefully. I noticed that city people weren't that different from us. Then we took the road to Fez, which went via Rabat. I must have been pretty tired because I slept almost all the way. When I woke up, I found Nabil's head resting on my shoulder. He was snoring lightly. I didn't move, so as not to disturb him. He hadn't slept a wink all night either. After Fez, we turned onto a small road that led to Imouzzer, a strange town where the houses had slanting roofs. The emir explained to us that winter was harsh in this region and these roofs allowed the snow to slide off. I thought that if there was a hole, it couldn't be plugged with branches or a plastic bag, because of the angle. We made our way to a thick forest, along bumpy tracks, and stopped in the middle of nowhere. We walked for a few hundred meters and suddenly came upon a lake. An impressive stretch of water, like a small sea imprisoned by possessive mountains. The emir said: "This is Dayt Aoua. The most beautiful place in the country." I thought to myself that besides his religious qualities, the emir was a poet, too. He had us take several tents out of the minibus and showed us how to put them up, using stakes. It was hilarious; we were helpless with laughter when our first attempts proved far from adequate. Eventually the emir gave us a hand and we organized a proper camp. Since we had to sleep two to a tent, Nabil and I naturally chose to share. Blackie objected because he didn't want to share with Fuad, claiming he snored, but he had no choice, since Hamid and Khalil had already paired up. We spread out our blankets. The shadows were so soft inside the tent I didn't want to leave it. Blackie was keen to light the fire. Even without coal, he managed it in no time at all. Most of us set about cooking the meal, as we were so hungry. And so began our holiday by the lake at Dayt Aoua.

The time we spent in the mountains will always be one of the happiest memories of my short life. I'd never seen so many trees in just one place; they were tall and majestic, their green branches caressed the scattered clouds. The emir knew all their names. He pointed out the umbrella pines; the eucalyptus, its bark streaked with sweet-smelling resin, whose roots could go very deep in search of water; and so many other kinds that lived serenely by the lake. We'd wake early in the morning. After prayers, which went on a long time, we'd make coffee and drink it together round the fire. We'd climb to the top of the mountain and do our exercises. That lasted several hours: warm-ups, kata, and combat. Then prayers and more prayers. Our exhausted bodies were at one with the sky, the earth, and the sparrows that dropped in to keep us company. We were so close to God and we could tell by their chirping that the birds felt it too. The more verses we recited, the louder they'd sing. And it all formed a kind of offering we'd humbly place at the feet of our Lord. As the emir finished his speech and, one after the other, we all took turns to insult Satan and his cronies, he'd ask us to follow him on interminable runs. We'd be out of breath but none of us could match his pace; we'd crawl back to camp. Khalil ran off toward the water and plunged in like a fish. The others all followed him in, yelling wildly, and I was envious because I couldn't swim. I'd just paddle and wet my face. Emir Zaid would see me on my own and come to sit down beside me on the bank and I'd listen rapturously to his accounts of the brave deeds of the Prophet and his companions.

On the third day, some friends of the emir joined us. We didn't know them, but they seemed to know us. They stayed with us all day and part of the evening and then left, returning at dawn the next morning. They trained, ran, ate, and prayed with us. We went for walks in the forest and friendships were formed. Initially, Jaber, a very tall man with a square face and gimlet black eyes, didn't seem at all trustworthy. And yet he was friendly and seemed almost apologetic about his massive build. He became my friend. Saad, his cousin, had a distinctive beard down to his belly button. He got on well with Nabil. The other two, whose names I've forgotten, teamed up with Khalil, Blackie, Fuad, and my brother Hamid. In a few sessions, Jaber taught us to handle a knife like the warriors in the days of the Jihad; he showed us the different positions to adopt in case of attack. And also how to anticipate a potential assault. The way to stick the blade in and which way to turn it; a twist of the wrist at a precise moment determined the degree of punishment inflicted on the infidel. We were exhilarated, and fully alert, because this was a matter of life and death. First we trained using reeds as knives, but by the end of the week we were fighting with real daggers. It was so exciting. We got a few scratches, but nothing serious. We were such good pupils that we were each given a knife of our own with a blade that flicked out from our sleeves if we pressed a button. It was a real gem; the knife I'd always dreamed of.

Night was quick to fall on Dayt Aoua. When the cicadas awoke, a black veil studded with jewels covered the mountains, the lake, the trees, and the birds' eyes. We'd gather round a campfire and sing praises to God. We'd pray and listen to the emir hold forth on the glorious epics of the past, on the battles we'd wage in order to raise the flag of Islam, which was constantly trampled underfoot all over the world, on the struggles the Lord demanded of us so that we might recover our dignity and restore our crumbling empire's prestige. And at the end lay paradise. As we went back to our tents to sleep, I saw, high up in the sky, split by a thin shaft of moonlight, an angel who was smiling at me.

In all this time, there was only one false note, which I deplore, because I let down my guard in the face of Satan's trickery. I ask God for forgiveness, because Nabil and I had sex. I'm not quite sure how it happened. We hadn't planned it, but there it was. To warm ourselves up, we'd huddled together in that tent where the ceiling was as low as a tomb's. I don't know if we were asleep, but our dulled minds were far away. The mountain air had something to do with it. Nabil's body brushing against mine gave me a shameful erection. He took my cock in his hand quite naturally and we kissed. We undressed and made love, without thinking. In silence. There, I've said it.

15

I KNEW HAMID so well that the day he took me off to the café to talk about *serious matters*, I told him my answer was yes before the words were even out of his mouth. He looked at me, his eyes filled with tears, and stammered: "We have no choice." I agreed, because someone had to make the sacrifice. That was the first time I'd ever seen dread in my brother's face. Here he was, the hero, the terror of Sidi Moumen, his voice breaking and his hands trembling. But I was calm. Maybe I hadn't yet grasped the gravity of the situation. Then that was it, we didn't talk about it again. I'd been the last to be told the date for the big event. A curious thing: none of my friends had refused to die. And yet dying was no small thing. Nabil, whom I'd thought was a coward, had said yes immediately, since he had no other ties besides us. He hadn't seen his mother in an eternity and was none the worse for it. He'd banned her from coming to the shack. It was an irrevocable decision, which he'd made in front of everyone. He'd publicly disowned her, cutting the cord once and for all. But Tamu didn't give up; she couldn't reconcile herself to losing her only son. She'd come and hang around near where we lived—it was a heartbreaking sight. Seeing her sitting near the pump with her cake on her knees, Nabil remained adamant. She was waiting for a kid to walk by, who'd bring us the cake. Nabil would refuse it and send it back to her, or he'd say to the kid: "Take it home, you can have it." Tamu looked on in silence. It didn't stop her coming back the next week with another cake and sitting down nearby. Nabil acted as if she didn't exist. He refused the baskets of food Abu Zoubeir gave us for our families, saying that he was an orphan. The master pretended to believe him, but the truth was he knew everything there was to know about us. Nabil would say that the day Tamu stopped selling her ass and repented of her sins, he'd think about it. He'd changed a lot. He'd hardened. His mother's profession was like a scar on his face. He was the son of Tamu. Tamu the whore. He was the son of a whore. The circle was complete. Even if no one talked about it, everybody thought it a bit. And there was that story that lingered on in the memory, gleefully repeated by all the old gossips. I don't know if it was true, but it had affected Nabil badly.

The day before he was born, his mother had taken a taxi to the hospital. As it was a long journey, she'd had time to talk to the driver, who was very chatty. When they arrived at the entrance, she asked him to help her carry her shopping bag, since she had to support her big belly, with the baby kicking about inside, impatient to see the light of day. The man agreed and helped her up the steps. At reception, the driver handed her back her bag and asked for the money for the ride.

Tamu barked: "What? You're leaving me?"

"Yes, madam, that's twenty dirhams."

"And your baby? What about your baby?"

"What baby are you talking about?"

"The one you shoved in my belly, you moron."

"I don't know you, lady. Is this a joke?"

Tamu put her hands over her ears and began to shout: "He's going to leave me. He's going to abandon his child. Call the police, this man is a coward!"

"You've lost your mind, woman. It's an asylum you need!"

Just as he was about to leave, giving up on the cab fare, the nurses restrained him until the arrival of the police, who immediately placed him in custody, in order to clarify the facts. His distraught family looked for him everywhere. He had a wife and three children, whom he loved. He led an easy life in the medina, since he was his own boss; he'd finished paying off the loan for his taxi and things were looking up. It was two days before his brother and his wife tracked him down at police headquarters. Then they were told the painful news: the man in question was living a double life. He'd impregnated a young woman who'd just given birth to a delightful boy, whose paternity he was denying. His wife fainted and they revived her. They were advised to hire a lawyer, since the poor girl was pressing charges from her hospital bed. That was how things began to get complicated. The lawyer reassured them that, these days, they had modern techniques to establish paternity. The DNA tests proved conclusive. Indisputable even: it turned out the driver had been sterile from birth. But he had three children, who looked like him—especially the eldest, who was his exact double. How was that possible? After much prevarication, his wife finally confessed. She loved her husband more than anything in the world. And since she'd realized he could not have children, and might reject her, she'd slept with his brother. But only so she would have children who'd bear a likeness to her husband. The driver was exonerated and, upon leaving the police station, he drove his taxi to the edge of a cliff and went straight over. So Nabil's birth was tainted by an appalling tragedy, which did not bode well for the future. When bad luck gets into you in your mother's womb, it never lets go. But it was no good my trying to explain to my friend that the blame lay with the people who'd cast us into this hole, that it wasn't Tamu's fault, because she'd had a child to feed, she was protecting herself as best she could, and ultimately she had no choice. He wouldn't listen to me. Or he'd just say: "We always have a choice." There was no way, then, to soften his heart.

Blackie hadn't batted an eyelid, either, when Abu Zoubeir made him the terrible proposition. He joked about how happy he'd be to leave, because he'd never have to see his father's miserable face again. But I knew he was suffering, he was tired of having his little brother's death on his conscience. He wanted to be rid of that burden, to win back the identity he'd been stripped of and be Yussef again. A Yussef as free as the air. Shed his skin, embrace nothingness, be born again, somewhere else . . .

Fuad had worried about Ghizlane, but he could not refuse Abu Zoubeir's invitation. It was an honor they were doing him. To be chosen as a martyr with the keys to paradise wasn't something bestowed on just anyone. But he wanted to be sure that his friends would look after his little sister. He was all she had in the world. Their grandmother didn't have long to live and Ghizlane would be all alone in Douar Scouila. Abu Zoubeir vowed that she would be protected, that he'd take care of her personally, as if she were his own daughter. That made us both feel better.

As for Khalil the shoeshine, he'd long wanted to get away. If he couldn't make it to Paris, Madrid, or Milan, because he risked getting his eyes eaten by crabs, he'd accept a one-way ticket to paradise. Maybe there he could become a crooner for the houris and the angels . . .

The two days before the big event went faster than anticipated. On no account were we to leave the garage by ourselves. We did a lot of praying. The idea of imminent death didn't dent our appetites. Like prisoners, we were entitled to better meals: tagine with cardoons and bitter olives, pigeon pastilla (a dish I'd only ever heard of), chicken with preserved lemons . . . They were so delicious that Emir Zaid, fearing that such marvels might make us regret leaving this world, made a point of saying that better meals, with flavors beyond compare, awaited us up above. He backed this up with one of the most joyous verses in the Koran.

The Oubaida brothers were at the training room to go over the last technical details. The paradise belts were ready and waiting. We met up with them at night for an initiation session. We tried on the vests and as mine was a bit tight, Fuad swapped it for his, because he was thinner. Sweat was running down Hamid's forehead and he looked at me in utter bewilderment. He couldn't understand why I was so calm, almost serene. Riding high, I saw the whole thing as a game; a game of life and death unwittingly entwined. Sidi Moumen's grim reaper was part of everyday life; she wasn't as frightening as all that. People came and went, lived or died, without it making the slightest difference to our poverty. Families were so big that losing one or two of their number was no catastrophe. That's how it was. We wept over our dead, of course, we buried them wailing and lamenting, but with the crowds of those still living there was so much to do that we soon forgot them. And yet, death was still there, everywhere. We had adopted her. She lived in us and we in her. She'd emerge from our red eyes and our clenched fists for brief sallies. She'd walk in white robes on the ruins of our shantytown and return to curl up inside us. We were the house she rested in and we'd find peace leaning on her. Death was our ally. She served us and we served her. We'd lend her our hatred, our vengeance, and our knives. She'd put them to good use and return them to us, only to demand them again. And again and again. She'd get us through the bad times, she'd haul us out of trouble, and we were so grateful to her. That night, in that ill-lit room, she was there to sustain me once more. I could feel her standing beside me, shivering. She was growing impatient. Her invisible presence had swallowed up all the people around me. I no longer saw them. I was alone with her and I wasn't afraid. She wrapped her black wings around my feverish body and I surrendered. I thought only of the joy of obedience. I was her slave, happy to belong to her. Death was thinking for me. All I had to do was follow the Oubaida brothers' instructions and everything would be fine. Bus number 31, the Genna Inn, and the cord I had to pull at the right moment. It wasn't complicated. She whispered those orders in my ear. Many times. I repeated the refrain in my head, to lodge it in my mind forever. Then, like an aging princess, she glanced over and pointed her finger at me. Death had singled me out from a horde of barefoot beggars, and I rejoiced to be among her chosen few. I was ready to give in to her every whim, provided she'd let me embrace her. Hang on tight and fly away with her. Traverse the seven heavens and be born again somewhere else, far away. As far away as possible from Sidi Moumen and its corrugated iron, its grime, and its rabble. Breathe new air, banish even the memory of the dump. Wallow in nothingness and put an end to boredom. Have done with mud and insects. Never again see kids in rags running after garbage trucks, fighting to be the first to scrabble around in the rubbish, sinking waist-deep in mounds of filth. No, never again did I want to see those monstrous machines vomit their refuse onto children.

Putting on that vest packed with explosives, I was already dust. That was a strange sensation. I formed one body with the earth, the sky, and the stars that strafed the black night. The sheikh's words scintillated in my mind and I felt invincible. No, you cannot defeat a man who wants to die. And I wanted to, fervently. Nabil, Blackie, Khalil, Fuad, and Hamid wanted to die too. Living in Sidi Moumen, surrounded by corpses, the groveling, and the lame, the truth was we were almost dead already. So really, what did it matter, a little more or less?

Hamid was still sweating and the Oubaida brothers were worried about him. They must have informed Abu Zoubeir. We left the training room and went to the hammam together. We washed ourselves and shaved our bodies closely, preparing ourselves for death as if for a wedding. We even made a few jokes about Nabil's backside; he was refusing to let anyone scrub him down. Fuad almost passed out when Emir Zaid brought us the clothes for the last night. The cleanest, whitest linen, which our bodies, purified of any stain, demanded.

On the way back to the garage, Abu Zoubeir took Hamid aside and they had a long conversation. My brother felt better after that. The master went back to his place in the middle of the room and prayed. Then he made a speech: "Remember that tonight, my children, many challenges await you. But you must confront them and understand them. The time for playing is over. The moment of judgment has arrived. So we must use these few remaining hours to ask God for forgiveness. You must recognize that there is almost no time left for you to live. Afterward, you will begin a life of bliss, of infinite paradise. Be optimistic. The Prophet was always optimistic. Pray, ask for God's help. Go on praying all night. You have vowed to die and you have renewed this oath for the love of God. This does you credit. Everyone hates death, I know; everyone fears it. But remember those verses that say that you would wish for death before meeting it, if you only knew of the reward that awaits you."

We recited other prayers, and Hamid's voice rose above the rest. He was swept away by the mystical mood of that extraordinary night, and his fervor bordered on trance. Was it fear, gnawing at his guts? No doubt, because he was sharper than us and he understood that there was no way back. It was too late to abandon ship; he knew too much. And so he'd set off, as we all had, with his hand on the holy Koran. Hamid was no traitor, neither to God nor to Abu Zoubeir, still less to me and the rest of the group. Maybe he was angry with himself for getting me involved in all this. I couldn't say. In any case, he wasn't himself anymore. His eyes were different. They no longer looked outward. I changed places with Fuad to be next to him. I wanted to reassure him, but he was elsewhere. The verses followed on from each other. And euphoria sprinkled its golden sand over our intoxicated minds. We thought only of paradise. We were basking in it already. It wouldn't be as hot and humid there as it was in the garage, because right now we were soaked to the skin. And there wouldn't be any bad smells either. I hate to say it, but Hamid smelled strongly of sweat. It wasn't like him; usually he was very clean. With the ritual ablutions we performed several times a day, it was really hard to be dirty. Whatever the truth, we remained side by side for a good part of the night. After dawn prayers, blankets were brought and we collapsed on the mats, exhausted, half dead.

I didn't dream at all.

16

WE AWOKE AT ten the next day. Abu Zoubeir had dark rings round his eyes, as if he hadn't slept. Emir Zaid had shaved off his beard during the night and appeared instantly younger. I hardly recognized him. He looked like a schoolboy handing his satchel to the master. They went off together to the back of the room and conferred in hushed tones for a while. They seemed preoccupied. Nouceir and the Oubaida brothers arrived later, having swapped their white gandouras for modern clothes: striped trousers and blue jackets, which made them look like triplets. They too had shaved and cut their hair. Blackie whistled when he saw them and we all laughed briefly. Nabil and Fuad were on their feet, still drowsy. Hamid seemed calmer than the night before. He tapped me on the shoulder and I was glad we were together again. We all had breakfast in the garage: bread, olive oil, and mint tea, with the right amount of sugar. He didn't say Yemma's name but we were both thinking about her. I wasn't very hungry and only ate out of greed, thinking that this was my last meal. Never had food tasted so good. A few rays of sun filtered through the tiny window over the door. It was going to be a beautiful day. A soothing voice chanted selected verses from the Koran, on cassette. We listened in silence. Every time the Prophet's name was uttered, murmurs of "Peace and salutations be upon Him" filled the room. In truth, our attention was more focused on our individual itineraries. All six of us would be going to the Genna Inn hotel, but in two groups. Fuad, Nabil, and me first, then Khalil, Blackie, and Hamid. Emir Zaid and his companions were set to leave the city on another mission. We washed and said a communal prayer, led by Abu Zoubeir. We were in a hurry to join the angels who'd be waiting for us once we'd taken the great leap, who'd look after us and lead us to God. Abu Zoubeir reminded us we should never stop saying our prayers, as Satan would attempt to save the godless using every trick in the book. His guile knew no bounds. He'd breathe doubt in our minds, he'd do anything to break our resolve. We were waging war in the name of God. We were His soldiers. The hour of Jihad was upon us. He congratulated us on being chosen by the Lord to

carry out His will. He said there was no reason to fear
the enemies of Islam, we had our fates and theirs at the
end of a string. We need only to pull on it to dispatch
them to hell. Allah is great! Allah is great!

We left the garage in small groups to go to the training room. The harsh sunlight blinded us and it took
us a while to get used to the tumult of the street with
all its colors. A man on a bike, with a little black boy
riding sidesaddle on the bar, crashed into Khalil. The
boy fell off and blood began streaming from his ear.
Khalil did not react, he apologized, though it was the
cyclist's fault. Under normal circumstances, the incident would have degenerated into a brawl, with the
whole neighborhood weighing in. Khalil helped the
stunned kid get to his feet and handed him back to his
father, who immediately went on his way. The dump
was crawling with people, as usual. Above the deaf-
ening drone of the garbage trucks, Oum Kalthoum's
haunting voice wailing from shop to shop, the everyday arguments, and the dogs barking, you could still
hear the Koran, which some lost blind men were reciting to move people to pity. They'd picked the wrong
part of town to beg in and were walking in single file,
holding on to each other's djellabas. The leader had a
stick, which he was waving wildly in the air because
kids were pestering him. I glanced at Hamid, who
smiled at me. We'd done the same at their age. But

now he shouted to scare off the little rascals. To my surprise, I found myself reciting the sura along with the blind men.

We passed near Omar the coalman's shop. Blackie stopped for a moment to kiss his father's head. The old man accepted his apologies and said that he could come back home; his mother was unhappy. "God willing!" he replied, but we knew that God had other plans for us. As for me, I was longing to go and see Yemma, to kiss her hands and feet, with that secret paradise beneath them. I'd have loved to spend a few moments with my father, whom I barely knew. I'd have hugged him, for the first and last time. Said would have bored me to tears, criticizing the Americans' iniquitous policies and their shameful United Nations veto, and I'd have pretended to understand world affairs. And while I was at it, why not drop in on Douar Scouila? I missed Ghizlane terribly. I'd have liked to take her in my arms and say how sorry I was for abandoning her. Sorry for the mute promises my eyes had made, for the vows my mouth had not spoken, which she'd understood all the same. Sorry for letting her brother get mixed up in this venture, when we could have done without his services. Six martyrs for just one place was too many. One would have been enough. But there had to be explosions in different parts of the hotel and at fifteen-minute intervals, to cause maximum damage. In any case, we'd had no say in the matter. The master's decisions were final, because he had them from God. I'm sure Ghizlane would have been glad to see me. She'd have prattled away and that would have made me happy. She'd have ridiculed my pretentious outbursts and I'd have kept on asking her forgiveness, on my knees, for everything I hadn't given her because the good Lord had laid claim to my flesh and blood. I'd have stolen one last kiss and trembled all over again. I'd have told her everything that was making my heart heavy, everything I hadn't been able to say, since the mutinous words wouldn't obey me: "I will love you forever, but I'm going, my love, I have no choice. How long must we put up with the humiliation and contempt, living like rats in Sidi Moumen? You see, it's all decided, I'm going to die. I will take revenge on those people who plundered your childhood and trampled your dreams in the dirt. I will make them pay an eye for an eye for the years of slavery they have made us endure. They will suffer as we have suffered. All those traitors who buried their heads in the sand, I'll yank them up and slit their throats as if they were sheep. Let their children cry the way we have cried. I am going, my love, but promise me you'll go on with your embroidery. You have a gift. I am sure that one day it will be recognized and you'll be able to make a decent living from your art. I know you're looking after Mi-Lalla, but you need to think of yourself, too. She's right, make sure you have a trousseau, because one day, a boy will come and ask for your hand. You must be ready. You'll make a go of it, as ever. Promise me you'll be happy, because you deserve to be. I don't want any harm to come to you. Anyway, you must know I'll always be with you. Even when I'm kissing the houris (now, don't be jealous!), I'll be thinking of you. I'll drink all the elixirs of paradise to your health. And I'll wait for you, because sooner or later we all die. I'm doing it early, for the cause, but there's no hurry for you. You can take your time, have children, watch them grow up. You'll give them the love you never had. I don't want them to live in Sidi Moumen, because there's no hope there. Satan's acolytes have crushed it. If you have a boy, call him Yachine. He's the best goalkeeper the world's ever known. That will bring him luck. I will wait for you in paradise, I swear. Then we'll be able to love each other and kiss, like we did the other night in the darkness, near your house. It felt so good, kissing you." I stopped my reverie there, as we weren't far from the training room.

Our orders were to follow each other at a distance, not to spread out, to speak to no one, but Emir Zaid and Abu Zoubeir looked the other way. They were walking behind, monitoring us discreetly.

At the training room, everything was ready. The Oubaida brothers had prepared the equipment meticulously. There were real explosive charges in the pockets of the vests. We'd done our initiation with bricks. That was why Emir Zaid advised us to be extremely careful. The Oubaida brothers explained to us that once the devices had been set, they were the only ones who could disconnect them. That gave me goose bumps. Abu Zoubeir hugged us one by one and we all hugged each other. I had tears in my eyes when Hamid put his arms around me. It was my turn to crack, but no one noticed. That said, all of our eyes were glistening. We kept reciting the Koran as we put on the vests, which the Oubaida brothers fastened carefully; we spat on Satan and his army of infidels and we went out to meet our destinies. Fuad, Nabil, and I were leaving first. The others would take the next bus. Emir Zaid and his friends escorted us to the wall and disappeared just as they'd come, one night in Sidi Moumen. So we were let loose in the wild like hungry wolves, ready to devour the entire planet.

17

THE DOORMAN OF the Genna Inn was wearing a hand-some red uniform with a marshal's gold stripes and a miniature fez on his head. He didn't notice me walk in because I'd dodged between the luggage porters, who were pushing a massive gilt trolley piled high with suitcases. Tourists as white as corpses came in at the same time. Fuad and Nabil were supposed to join me a few minutes later, so as not to arouse the suspicions of the security guards. The glass door spun round and round like a carousel. And suddenly, the light . . . An orgy of bulbs glittered in an immense hallway; you'd have thought you were already in the paradise Abu Zoubeir had rhapsodized about. Perched on high heels, bare-backed virgins walked this way and that over the smooth floor, which was so clean it gleamed. I couldn't tear my eyes away from the shoes gliding all around me, of every color, polished, made exclusively for this kind of surface. And the music! A succession of light, delicate notes, so different from the racket of our tam-tams and crotales, flitted through the perfumed air as if each of them was borne by a cherub. Studied laughter swelled here and there and slowly subsided, caressing my ears, almost making me forget I was about to die. So I'd entered the antechamber of that other world, which held out its arms to me, whispering so many promises. I wondered at that point if I'd already activated the device wrapped round my chest. My heart nearly stopped when a security guard came over to find out what I was up to. I replied that I was waiting for my boss and he let me be, but kept his eye on me all the same. I looked through the plate-glass window that had a view of the garden. Virgins with bare breasts, their sex hardly concealed by a triangle of cloth the size of a vine leaf, were basking in the sun on funny-looking beds, in the shade of brightly colored parasols; others swam in an expanse of water so transparently blue it looked as if the sky had tipped into it. A clump of date palms rose up from the middle of the pool, to the delight of the birds. On the right, up three steps, stretched the restaurant. Tables covered in white cloths, on which sat floral-patterned plates, round glasses, and silver cutlery. The whole display sparkled in the sun, an invitation to a feast. The grilled meat smelled so good. My heart did not stop pounding because the guard had come back and was giving me a dirty look. But I was smartly dressed and my espadrilles were spanking new. I was wearing a loose jacket and a pair of jeans, lent to me by Hamid. When I saw the guard coming toward me, I clutched at the cord, in spite of the emir's strict orders: surround yourself with the maximum number of infidels before you pull. But the guard walked straight past me, heading for a guest who was calling to him. I took a deep breath. Fuad and Nabil were a long time coming. Those few minutes seemed an eternity. I sat down on a sofa and instantly gave a start, I was so unused to it: I felt I was being sucked into the void. A dog as small as a cat came and sat by my feet, as if I'd stepped in some dog mess. I'd never seen such a creature, with long hair, all silky curls. He was nothing like the strays at the dump. You could hardly see his face. I gave him a subtle kick under the table to get rid of him; he yelped and was off. His mistress ran to pick him up, clasped him to her large breasts, and stroked him, looking me up and down. I acted dumb and averted my eyes, but the old woman kept turning round as she walked off—there was just me on the sofa, and her dog wasn't the type to yelp for no reason.

I was relieved to see Nabil enter the lobby. I signaled to him to walk slowly because of the slippery floor. In those clothes, with his chestnut hair and graceful walk, he could have been one of the hotel guests. He behaved normally, skirting a young woman who was sitting behind a table and seemed to be advising people. He walked past me, acting as if he didn't know me, and paused for a moment near the restaurant, where foreigners were sitting at tables, though it was early afternoon. Maybe that was their custom. Unless in these places people were so rich they never stopped eating. I thought that as paradises go, this one would suit me just fine. There was no need to go right up in the sky to be happy. Snacking all day long and sprawling in the shade, surrounded by gorgeous sirens, would do for me. Satan had already started to undermine me, complicate my job, stop me from pulling the cord, so that he'd save the godless. Nabil was growing impatient; Fuad hadn't showed. We were starting to worry about him. A westerner walked past my friend, eyeing up his backside. I thought to myself that even here Nabil's ass would cause aggravation.

Behind a gleaming mahogany desk, two men dressed to the nines were greeting the tourists. Their smiles weren't like ours. They seemed false, because it's impossible to smile all day long, even when you're happy. They must have had a lot of training to make their cheeks move like that, but the rest of their face remained expressionless. The tourists seemed to have no problem with these fixed grins and made a similar face themselves as they went about filling in forms. Watching their kids playing around the suitcases, I thought of the young Palestinian boy who'd died in his father's arms. As soon as the loop started in my head, I stood up and walked toward them, advancing like a sleepwalker. I was myself and someone else at the same time. I noticed the tiniest details, as if my mind had suddenly woken up and entered a higher dimension. I looked over toward the entrance, but there was still no sign of Fuad. The doorman was still at his post and the future corpses were still pushing the revolving glass door. Time was passing and the tension was mounting. It was possible that Fuad had panicked and fled into the backstreets of Casablanca. Nabil must have been thinking the same thing because, as he came up to the desk, he nodded. That "yes" froze the blood in my veins, because it meant it was time to act. When he disappeared into the restaurant, my heart was thudding so hard I thought it would burst. Sweat ran down my forehead as I said my prayers; my trembling hand gripped the cord as if it were a lifeline. I was wrestling with Satan, who, by some diabolical trick, had turned the blond kids playing near the suitcases into the Palestinian boy who'd died in his father's arms. I muttered a sura under my breath, then louder and louder, but the kids were still Palestinian. I squeezed the cord between my fingers but some evil force stopped me from pulling it. Then I saw the security guard approaching from a long way off with a determined look on his face; I knew he was coming for me. He was an inch from grabbing me when the explosion reverberated through the restaurant. Then I saw nothing, because I was catapulted through the air, blown away by another explosion, along with all the tourists around me. The guard, too, exploded into a thousand pieces, along with the little dog and the old bag carrying him, the guys behind the desk and their fixed grins. I'd pulled the cord inadvertently, because Satan's cunning had almost triumphed, in spite of all my prayers. It was tough, very tough, hearing the children's laughter, seeing their hands and their eyes and their guardian angels dangling from the thread I held. I was like a puppeteer. I had their destinies at my fingertips. Yes, it was butchery, it was hell. It was the end of the world. There was more carnage ten minutes later when the second group entered the hotel. The doorman, who tried to block their path, was stabbed by Hamid and the firework display went on, decimating survivors and rescuers, sowing desolation and chaos: smoke, flames, dust, the debris of furniture and bodies; screams, still more screams, from the wounded and the survivors, and the groans of the dying who weren't lucky enough to die quickly; groans that echoed in many tongues, though the sobbing had no color and no country. The sobbing of human beings lying on the ground, stunned, dazed, lost. And people scrambling in all directions, terrified of another explosion.

Yes, we'd succeeded beyond all expectations. Abu Zoubeir, Emir Zaid, and his companions must have been rubbing their hands in front of their television sets. Fuad must have been tearing through the Casablanca streets like a convict, with his bomb pressing on his heart, searching all over for the Oubaida brothers to disconnect it. As for us, we were dead, just dead.

And I'm still waiting for the angels.

18

FROM THE DEPTHS of my solitude, when memories of my ruin assail and torment me, when the weight of my faults becomes too heavy to bear and my mind, already old and tired, begins to spin like an infernal merry-go-round, when Yemma's tears fall on me like a shower of fire and Ghizlane's grief injects its deadly poison into my soul, I go off wandering in the sky of my childhood.

I often go there at night to watch the shifting shadows take possession of the place, as the last lights go out. Then I weep, in my own way, waiting for daybreak. The slum hasn't changed. It's grown even bigger, and the shacks that were once separate now form a city. A vast city of the living dead. I wait and I cry, watching the wheel that keeps on turning. The dump is there, eternal and infinite. In the writhing turmoil of the garbage

Mahi Binebine

trucks, the foragers and the seagulls, the herds of goats munching on plastic bags, the dogs and cats shrouded in gray smoke and dust clouds, I can see some scrawny kids running after a flat ball, without a care in the world: the new Stars of Sidi Moumen.

ACKNOWLEDGEMENTS

The translator wishes to thank Ros Schwartz, Rémi Labrusse, Babajide Oyenigba, and especially Amia and Mahi Binebine for all their help.

MAHI BINEBINE was born in Marrakesh in 1959. He studied in Paris and taught mathematics until he became recognized first as a painter, then as a novelist. Binebine lived in New York in the late 1990s, when his paintings began to be acquired by the Guggenheim Museum. His first novel, *Welcome to Paradise*, was published in France by Librairie Artheme Fayard in 1999, in Great Britain in 2003 by Granta Books, and in the Unites States in 2012 by Tin House Books. He lives in Marrakesh.

LULU NORMAN is a writer, translator, and editor who lives in London. She has translated Albert Cossery, Mahmoud Darwish, Tahar Ben Jelloun, and the songs of Serge Gainsbourg and written for national newspapers, the *London Review of Books*, and other literary journals. Her translation of Mahi Binebine's *Welcome to Paradise* (Granta, 2003; Tin House Books, 2012) was short-listed for the Independent Foreign Fiction Prize. She also works as editorial assistant of *Banipal*, the magazine of modern Arab literature.